Other books

by

John Dellinger

Quigly's Dilemma

Dinosaur Tracks and Murder

11-24-96
To Dave
Merry
Christmas
John
Dellugli

Homecoming

to

Murder

HOMECOMING
to
MURDER

John Dellinger

Lone Wolf Publishing
Denver, Colorado

Lone Wolf Publishing

Homecoming to Murder

PRINTING HISTORY
First Printing 1996

ISBN: 0-937693-05-7

PRINTED IN THE UNITED STATES OF AMERICA.

by BookCrafters Inc.

10 9 8 7 6 5 4 3 2 1

One

Nineteen fifty-three was a bad year and a good year rolled into one. It started like the previous two years had started, very bad, with the war in Korea being the major obstacle to my happiness and well-being. Then it had turned good with the ending of the war on July 27. As I rolled home on the train on a September night, starting the journey in Los Angeles and expecting to end it in Denver, I had no idea the year would continue the pattern of good and bad. It was like Colorado's fall weather, one minute sunny and warm and the next blowing snow and freezing.

I could have flown home, but I was in no hurry. The

clackity clack sound of the train rolling through the night was good. It was a peaceful sound, with a steady comforting swaying, almost rocking me to sleep. I sat in coach and most of the other occupants of the car had taken pillows from the porter and were sound asleep, their heads buried in the soft white pillows as they leaned back in their seats.

No one sat next to me, and that was good. I wanted as little human contact as possible. Maybe other passengers wanted to avoid me because of the Marine-green uniform, with the rows of ribbons, I wore. Three stripes up and two stripes down, a Marine Corps gunnery sergeant was something most people avoided. Then again, maybe they just wanted to forget the war most had never known existed in the first place. But I couldn't forget. The gentle rocking of the train and the quiet night, with people sleeping all around me, gave me the time to remember the war that nobody wanted to remember.

This was my second homecoming from war. The first was World War II where I had ended up in a hospital after being carried off the island of Iwo Jima. We had raised the flag on that one and our side had won the war. Korea was different. There were no victory parades. Some thought we had lost the war, but we hadn't. We just hadn't won it, and that wasn't our fault. It was the fault of politicians and the real tragedy was that nobody gave a damn. Nobody wanted to remember us or the war. It was over and the American public wanted to forget it like it had never been.

Maybe I had been a fool to rush to enlist in this one. Martin Mayfield, private investigator, I had wanted to stop the Communists. This was the test of wills between the Communist world and the free world. When Communist North Korea had attacked South Korea on June 25, 1950, I went to the Marine Corps recruiting station, an old World War II re-tread, answering the call to colors again. Maybe I wasn't totally old then at the age of 31. Now, at 34, I knew

I was old.

If there was a next war, I would sit it out. All I wanted to do was return to Denver and my private detective business. I wanted a bourbon and water with my feet propped up on my desk. I wanted a full-bodied woman in my arms and a .38 in my shoulder holster. I wanted it to be like it had been before Korea. I guess I wanted to forget the Korean War too, but in the night with the train swaying back and forth it was all too easy to remember.

We had gone ashore at Inchon September 15, 1950, after our side had been pushed into a pocket at the end of the five-hundred-mile Korean peninsula. General MacArthur had gone for an end run, sending the First Marine Division by sea up the west coast of Korea to Inchon. Having been a Marine sergeant, three stripes, in World War II and with the Corps desperately in need of trained NCO's to fight in the unexpected war in Korea, I had gone back into the line with almost no training. It had helped that I had known my company commander in World War II when he was a young lieutenant platoon commander. He started the Korean War as a captain and in command of our company.

As the train rocked, I could see the fifteen-foot sea wall, boulders piled on boulders, that we had gone over with wooden ladders at Inchon when we had come out of the landing craft from the sea. I could see the fighting advance to Seoul that had taken over a week. We took back the South Korean capital in house-to-house fighting. We kicked the Korean Communist army out and put them on the run, but it had been costly. In two weeks of fighting, our company had sustained over fifty-percent casualties, most of them wounded, a great many of them killed.

The company commander didn't make it home this time. He was killed at Seoul. I was lucky in this one. After three years I was coming home in one piece, having never been wounded. I still had my scar from Iwo Jima. Maybe that was enough.

Normally, I didn't like officers, but the company commander, who had been killed so early in the war, had been a good one, as was Colonel Lewis "Chesty" Puller who was in command of our regiment. I didn't mind officers if they bled and died like the rest of us. Colonel Puller, later General Puller, was willing to risk his share of the blood and we had confidence in him.

We boarded ships again after Seoul, and then after having the G.I. runs for a week, landed and joined the Army in pushing the North Koreans all the way to the Chinese border. We heard we were going home by Christmas. That was General MacArthur's pledge to us. We heard it in the ranks: "Tell the boys for me, they're going home when they reach the Yalu."

Well, it wasn't that easy. The Chinese Communists hit us with everything they had when we neared the Yalu River, the border between Korea and China. The Thanksgiving turkey was hardly out of our mouths when those damn Chinese bugles blew and they hit us in human-wave attacks. We were outnumbered as much as twenty to one, but they didn't make good on their orders to destroy the First Marine Division. They cut our supply lines and we would retreat, but we would retreat as Marines. We retreated for seventy-eight miles and we fought them wherever they had the will to fight. We came out with our dead, our wounded, and our equipment. We came out as Marines.

It was "Frozen Chosin", all right. Even though beads of sweat broke out on my forehead as I remembered the war, I could feel the gnawing cold of "Frozen Chosin" where the retreat had begun. We were on the west side of the huge reservoir with the winds from Siberia blowing snow across the ice.

Chesty Puller's First Marines, we were the rear guard on what our commanding general called an attack in a different direction. Powder-grain snow hit us in the face like specks of sand. Temperatures dropped to twenty degrees below zero. We climbed hills beside the narrow mountain road to kick the ChiComs off them so that we could pass by. I could hear the heavy breathing as we used M-1 rifles as canes, barrel up and the butt down, to steady our balance as we moved our frozen feet up the steep snow-covered hills.

Then there was the pop, pop of grenade launchers we attached to the M-1's to lob grenades into the enemy. The BAR's rattled as they unloaded magazines of twenty bullets in bursts of three or four bullets at a time into the ChiComs. Blow your bugles, you Chinese Communist bastards, and we'll go on kicking your ass every time you get near us.

I was sweating heavily as I remembered the flaming napalm our Marine corsairs dropped on the ridges and hills, burying the enemy in balls of fire in a frozen hell of snow. I remembered the gratitude I felt for those fighter pilots as they returned to help us again during those long, cold, weary days.

The enemy blew a bridge to trap us, but our cargo planes dropped steel spans by parachute, and we were on our way in a matter of hours. We stacked our frozen dead like logs of firewood in the backs of trucks and on trailers pulled by jeeps. The wounded huddled in trucks when there was room. Those of us who could walk and whose feet hadn't been totally stopped by frostbite kept our feet moving as best we could until the next attack by the ChiComs.

The ChiComs were hurting too. They surrendered in increasing numbers, frozen and bloody like we were. When we finally reached the port of Hungnam, after five days of a fighting retreat, we had our dead, our wounded, long lines of prisoners, and a staggering number of Korean refugees who were fleeing Communist North Korea with as much as they could carry.

My pulse rate lessened and I was sweating less as I remembered sailing away from the North Korean coast. My pulse rate went up as I remembered being thrown back into the line again in South Korea. We took Seoul again and peace talks began and then broke off.

Sweat broke out all over my forehead as I remembered the Punchbowl and Heartbreak Ridge. Heartbreak was 3,900 feet above sea level and we lost a lot of good men, Marines and Army, taking Heartbreak and other ridges. With vegetation blown away, leaving only dirt, it hardly seemed worth a nickel, much less the lives of good men.

Then peace talks again dragged on and on. They wouldn't let us fight an offensive war. We lived in trenches like rats, sending out patrols and fighting skirmishes. What did the politicians know about war? Americans were fighters who attacked and won. We were ass-kickers, but they made us trench rats and wouldn't let us win. Our orders were to hold what we had. "Conduct only limited actions for limited gains." And the peace talks droned on for months as men continued to die.

The war had ended almost where it had begun. Three years, one month, and two days, and all we had to show for it was the same field position the South Koreans had held when they had been attacked by the North Koreans. We had stopped the Communists from taking South Korea, but North Korea was still swaggering and threatening across the border.

Well, I was on my way home. The politicians could have their damn political wars that ended with the other guy still standing. Personally, I liked for all of my fights to end the same way, with the other guy hurt so bad that he was never going to come at me again.

I bolted from my seat, bumping the leg of a man who had his leg out in the aisle as I headed for the club car. Startled from his sleep, he started to say something. I stopped and glowered at him, wanting nothing more than a fight, to smash something, anything. He checked what he started to say and looked frightened.

When I reached the club car I sat at the bar and barked at the bartender, "Give me a bourbon and water! Keep 'em coming until I tell you to stop."

"Yes, sir," the colored bartender said, obviously aware that I was upset.

He hastily poured the drink and set it in front of me. "Sergeant, you want more, I'll keep pouring. If there's anything I can do for you, let me know. If you drink it slow," he said softly, "it will last longer."

I started to bark at him again, but then I gained control of myself. "Yeh, I guess you're right," I said calmly. I knocked the bourbon and water back and put the empty glass on the counter. "I'll go easy on the next one. It just feels like it's been a long time between drinks."

"Going home?" he asked as he set the next one in front of me.

"I sure am."

"I see a lot of you fellows on this train. Most of 'em don't even wear their uniforms. It don't seem right somehow, what you all did and so few people saying much about it. My son, he got back last week from the Army. He didn't even wear his uniform home, and him a corporal. That's pretty good for him just being twenty, ain't it, Sergeant?"

"That's damn fine. If he did a hitch and got out a corporal, he did O.K. Was he in Korea?"

"Yes, sir, but I don't know where. He won't tell me a thing."

"Well, he was my brother in arms," I said, lifting my glass. "Here's to your kid, pop, and all the other fine men who served in Korea. May all of us miserable bastards forget the war and get on with our lives, but let us never forget our buddies who died there."

I drained the glass. "Hit me again, pop. I'll go slow on the next one. Hell, I haven't paid for the first two yet. I guess I'm not thinking too good tonight." I started to reach for my money belt, tied under my shirt around my waist. I had my mustering-out pay and I had carefully stashed it in anticipation of my trip home.

"Keep your money, Sergeant."

I looked over my shoulder at the nun who spoke. I had noticed her sitting at the table by the bar on my way in, but I had been too damn mad to pay much attention or think of how incongruous it was to see a nun in her black habit, sitting at a table near a bar. It looked like she had a drink sitting in front of her.

"I'll pay for your drinks, if you let me," she continued. "You sound like you could do with some company, and so could I. There aren't too many people up at this time of night.

"That's very kind of you," I said, using my most civilized tone and moving from the bar to her table. I sat down in the chair opposite her and gave her a curious look.

"Do nuns always buy Marines drinks? Are you sure you are old enough to wear that thing?"

"I'm 27, so I can assure you I am old enough to wear whatever I choose. As to how I have enough money to buy you drinks, my father always supplied me with whatever money I needed. It is not coming out of the budget of the Little Sisters of Charity. You are obviously upset about something, so I feel it is my sisterly duty to see if I can calm you down before you get drunk enough to hurt someone. As to why I'm sitting here at 2:30 in the morning, I couldn't sleep. As you can see, there are only two other people in here besides us, so I thought even a nun could slip in for a quick one without being noticed. Any other questions, or have I answered them all?"

"Just one, do sisters have names?"

She hesitated and then said, "Sister Brochetti." She repeated it as if it was a satisfaction to hear her voice say it.

"Now, wild Marine, who are you?"

"Martin Mayfield, gunnery sergeant, U.S. Marine Corps, as of the day before yesterday. Today, I'm a civilian, still wearing my uniform. When I get back to Denver I'll take off this uniform, hang it in the closet, look at it every year or two and remember what it was like to fight a war that nobody gave a damn about, except those of us who fought it."

"Self pity doesn't become you. I thought Marines were tough."

"Ouch; that one hurt." I managed a slight smile as I reached for the pack of Luckies I carried in my left sock. That way the cigarette pack didn't bulge in your pocket and make you look sloppy. Marines were never supposed to look sloppy when they weren't in combat. "But I guess you're right. War's over and done." I knew it wouldn't be that easy to brush away three years of blood and guts, but I would try. "So, where is Sister Brochetti going?" I asked and then lit my cigarette with the Zippo lighter that had a gold-looking anchor and globe on it next to the silver-looking metal.

"Denver. May I have one of those?"

"What?"

"A cigarette."

"Sure, sister, whatever you say," I said while shaking a Lucky out of the pack for her. I held the lighter for her and watched her inhale greedily.

"You're no ordinary sister."

"Priests smoke, damn it. Why can't sisters?" she snapped.

"O.K. with me," I said, finding her more interesting by the minute. She had an attractive face with olive-black eyes. I could see a few strands of black hair sticking out from under her hood or whatever they called those things. I way trying not to get interested in her as a woman, but it had been a long war and she wasn't coming on as your typical nun. Her drinking rum and coke didn't correspond with what I thought they did at a nunnery. I wondered if I had been away from the states that long.

I couldn't get any personal information out of her except that she was going to Denver. She was quite familiar with the Little Sisters of Charity in Los Angeles and was willing to give me a history of the order. As to her personal role or part in the order, I could get nothing. If she had a family other than the father she had mentioned earlier, I couldn't get her to mention it and she made no further mention of him. I suspected she had something to hide. I wondered if she was running away from the nunnery.

"How tall are you?" she asked abruptly after her third drink and second cigarette.

"A little over six feet!"

"Nice blue eyes, dark blue like a deep lake. Your black hair would probably look a little better of you let it grow more. Your complexion looks almost Italian; of course, my father was blue-eyed and lighter skinned. My mother was dark-eyed and typical Southern Italian. Both of their families came from Sicily, but somehow my father ended up looking more Northern Italian than Sicilian.

I said nothing, trying to make out what this was all about as she looked at her empty glass as if trying to decide whether to have another.

"How much do you weigh?" she continued.

"Oh, about 190. I'm a little heavier than when I went back into the Corps. Strange that I could gain weight in a war. Most guys lose it. Must have been that Marine Corps chow and almost no booze for three years."

She stood up. "Would you walk me back to my compartment?"

I quickly agreed, flattered at the offer. I threw a buck on the bar for the bartender. He thanked me for the tip and I could see a questioning look in his eye as the nun started to walk away. He said in a low voice, barely above a whisper, as he picked up the dollar bill, "You be careful, Sergeant, be real careful."

"Sure, pop," I said as I started to follow the nun. I knew there was a great deal that was strange about this nun. After surviving three years of the Korean War I wasn't about to be rolled by a nun. As I followed behind her I tried not to think carnal thoughts about the body that was under the habit. About five-five, I guessed she would have an attractive figure. I shook my head, trying to clear it of such thoughts as I thought about how pretty her face was. She reminded me of one of my favorite movie stars, Loretta Young.

We stopped at her compartment. I expected her to thank me and I would return to my seat in coach. Instead, she said, "Come in, please."

I followed her in and when she switched on the light, she caught me with my left arm out, searching for another occupant of the car.

She smiled. "Really, Sergeant, did you think I was going to have someone waiting to hit you over the head and steal your money?"

"Well, you've got to admit, you are a little different for a nun."

She looked up at me with a teasing look. "Ever kiss a nun?" She pushed the hood back off her head, and full-bodied, fluffy black Italian hair fell onto her shoulders.

I accepted the invitation and pulled her to me in a tight embrace and long kiss. "But you're a nun," I said as I pulled my face back and looked down at her.

"Even priests probably need it once in awhile," she said in a teasing tone. "Let's just say you got lucky. Besides, if I were really a nun, do you think I would be acting this way?"

"But if you're not a nun, why are you masquerading as one?"

"No more questions, Sergeant, or I'll ask you to leave. It is enough that I've invited you in. Do you want it or don't you?"

She didn't have to ask twice. She was as full-bodied as I had imagined she would be. The closeness of her body, coupled with the rocking movement of the train, gave me my first relief from the war in over three years.

When it was over, she made me leave. "Obviously, Sergeant, I don't want my ruse as a nun discovered. Gentlemen don't talk. You just got lucky tonight; maybe I was feeling patriotic, lonely or something. Then again, I shouldn't drink; it loosens me up too much. Have a happy civilian life and forget this ever happened. If you talk about this, I could be in danger. Please just be gratefully quiet about it."

"Want to tell me about it?" I asked. "Marines are tough. I might be able to help."

"No. Our secret, O.K.?"

"O.K., " I said. "Thanks, princess. That's about the nicest homecoming a guy could have. If you need anything in Denver, let me know. My name isn't in the telephone book yet, but in civilian life I'm a private detective. Just call information and ask for Martin Mayfield, Private Investigations. I'll have it listed in a day or two. My business cards seem to have gotten lost in the Korean War."

She laughed lightly amid a smile. "Wouldn't you know it? I take in a poor lonely Marine and he turns out to be a private snoop. Well, don't let your curiosity get the best of you. If I need anything, I'll call, but don't sit by the telephone and wait."

When I returned to my seat in coach I had no trouble sleeping. I dozed contentedly into the next afternoon, ignoring the people walking up and down the aisle, noisy kids, and chattering daytime conversation. I arrived at Denver needing a shave and a shower, with a mouth that needed its teeth brushed and a swirl of mouthwash. My uniform was crumpled. Already I was starting to look like a civilian. ‘Sister Brochetti’ was nowhere to be seen as I got off the train.

Two

I took a taxi to the Pig and Poke, but I had the driver wait when I saw the place was empty. I had intended to get my old room back in the motel at the back of the restaurant, but Frank Brodrick and none of the help seemed to be on the premises. A little handwritten note, scrawled on a paper on the front door of the restaurant said, "Closed for the funeral". The scrawl looked like Ida's, Frank's long-time waitress, so I assumed she was still working there. I hopped back into the yellow cab and had the driver run me about a half-mile further up the street to Galliger's Car Lot.

Joe Galliger was sitting in his front office, looking out a plate glass window, probably waiting for a sucker to browse his rows of used cars. He spotted me immediately as I stepped out of the cab. So fast was his exit from his office that the stub of a black cigar that he had been smoking dropped from his lips as he hit the black asphalt after coming down the three wooden steps, painted blue, that led to his office.

"Marty, Marty," he said, throwing his pudgy arms around me. "Welcome home." He hugged me and in his excitement even planted a kiss on my cheek.

The cab driver looked at us as if we might be a little funny.

"It's O.K.," I said to the cab driver. "He's a friend of mine."

"Friend, hell," Joe said. "Marty, you know damn well you're like a son to me."

The cab driver looked less accusing and waited to be paid his fare. He was smiling as if he was enjoying the warmth of the reunion.

I shook Joe's hand and said, "See what happens when a guy never marries and has no family of his own; he adopts stray Marines."

"This bum, not one letter or word from him in three years. You might have been dead for all we knew. Thanks to Delana, we did find out that you were in Korea. She kept tabs on you from her sources. We knew you weren't showing up on the casualty reports, so we figured you were still alive."

"That's what reporters are supposed to do, find out things. How is she?"

"Fine, and I still think she's carrying the torch for you."

"I hate to break this up," the cab driver broke in, "but my dispatcher will be on my ass if I'm out of the cab too long."

"Sure, pal," I said. "Joe, pay the man, will you?" I reached into the back seat to pull out my green sea bag as Joe reached for his wallet.

"Joe grumbled, "Gone three years and the first time I see him, he stiffs me for the cab fare."

"Tip the man too, Joe. He had to wait while you slobbered over me."

Joe smiled, handing the driver a five. "Keep it," he said, which was uncharacteristic of Joe. "You in the market for any kind of a personal vehicle yourself?" Joe continued, which was very characteristic of Joe.

"Not at the moment, but thanks for the tip."

The cab driver retreated quickly, wanting to escape before Joe could give him a sales pitch. Joe stopped him from driving away by placing a hand on the wiper blade in front of the driver. "Your windshield wiper looks pretty worn. That's the kind of thing we keep an eye out for here at Galliger's You come to Galliger's Car Lot and we check our cars out thoroughly."

The driver said, "I'll remember that," and stepped on the gas, leaving Joe no choice but to let go of the wiper blade. We watched the cab drive away.

"Business that bad, Joe, that you have to attack taxi drivers?"

"No, actually it's been pretty good. But, you never know unless you ask. That's what being a salesman is all about, putting your product in front of the public. How come you are coming home so broke that I've got to pay your cab fare?" Get rolled by a chippy?"

"No. I've got money. I just didn't want to drag my money belt out in front of that cab driver. I'll give you your five when we get inside."

When we were inside and sitting in Joe's customer chairs, Joe wouldn't take the five back, which was pretty unusual for him. He said it was my homecoming present.

"Pretty rough war, Marty?"

"Nah, hell, a piece of cake. On the way up here I noticed that the Pig and Poke was closed. How come?"

"Frank Brodrick's funeral. Tomorrow at 10 a.m. at the Chapel of Memories up the street. They are going to plant him in Crown Hill."

Joe looked sad and I was sad too. Frank was a good friend. "What happened, heart attack?"

"He should have been so lucky. Somebody blew his head off with a shotgun."

"I'll be damned. Was it robbery? Frank kept quite a bit of money at the Pig and Poke."

"Doesn't appear to be. It happened in a tunnel at the new coliseum."

"What coliseum?"

"While you were gone they built a new facility to house the National Western Stock Show. It has become such a big thing that the old facility couldn't take care of all the animals and spectators. Frank's body was found in some kind of a tunnel out there. That's about all I know about it."

"Harry Makris still around?"

"As far as I know. I haven't seen him in a couple of months, but the last I heard he was still on the police force."

"Well, I'll get him to fill me in on the details. Damn, Joe, I hardly expected one of my friends to be murdered when I came home. Looks like I've got my first case. Nobody has hired me, but Frank deserves that much from me."

Joe paused in lighting the cigar as if to say something, but then went ahead pulling air through the fresh black cigar before the wooden match he had struck went out. The cigar burned easily, and black, strong-smelling smoke started to fill the office. "You want me to hire you, Marty? Frank was my friend too. I'd like to see whoever killed him caught."

"That won't be necessary. I've got my mustering-out pay. I sent money to Frank to bank for me when I was in Korea. He once told me something about old fighters ending up broke and down and out. He said I ought to put aside something for my old age. I started giving him a little money to pay my rent in advance and to run a tab on my food in advance. When I went back into the Marine Corps so unexpectedly I just took out a fifty-dollar-a-month allotment and had it sent to Frank. I figured he would bank it for me and then I'd have someplace to live and eat when I came home, no matter what shape I came home in."

"Jeez, Marty, that's $1800 in three years. I hope it is in a bank or something. Too bad you didn't send it to me, but Frank would have taken real good care of it for you. He wouldn't have cheated you."

"Frank was a real straight shooter," I said while standing up. "My office still vacant or did your rent it out? If you didn't rent it out, I've still got a bottle of bourbon in the drawer. Let's have a drink to Frank and to my homecoming."

"It cost me, but I didn't rent it to anybody else. It's just like you left it. Your name is still on the door. If you would have been killed, I would have rented it, but I knew you would be back if you could."

We went to the little office that sat off to the side of Joe's little white frame house next to his car lot. The office had been used by Joe when he was first getting started in the car business before he had built the business enough to put in the office he now used. 'MARTIN MAYFIELD- PRIVATE INVESTIGATIONS' was still in black letters on the glass window in the top of the door. The letters looked so good I almost cried as I looked at them while Joe went into his house to get the key to my office. It had been a long war and I was glad to be back.

After Joe unlocked the door and handed me the key I pulled open the deep right desk drawer and took out the bottle of never-opened Kentucky bourbon that was where I had left it three years before. I had promised myself I would drink it on my return. I set the fifth on the desk and pulled out two of the six glasses I kept in the drawer for myself and guests. They were your typical restaurant water glasses.

"These glasses could probably use a rinsing out," I said as I went to the white wall sink and tried to turn on the water. Nothing came out of the faucet."

"What did you expect, Marty? You been gone three years and you didn't expect me to turn the water off?"

"Yeh, I guess you're right," I said, pouring the glasses half full and handing one to Joe. "We'll drink it straight." I raised my glass. "To Frank Brodrick."

"To Frank," Joe said as he raised his glass, "and to your homecoming."

"And my homecoming," I agreed. I took a long pull at the bourbon and Joe took a light swallow. He was 56-years-old and it was during business hours, so I assumed he was going easy on the booze.

"You don't have to drink the rest of it," I said to him.

"You ever see an Irishman waste good whiskey?" he asked, tipping the glass back and splashing a little of the bourbon on his gray, wide eyebrows as he drained the glass. "So, my nose is a little red, what the hell. I'm the boss, ain't I? I can have a drink if I want to."

"Where's Smitty today?"

"I sent her out to order some flowers for Frank's funeral. I've got another salesman who comes on at five. I've only got him working nights and weekends. I'd better get back up front since I'm all alone. You can use the house to clean up. Your clothes are still in those boxes you packed them in before you left. They are sitting in the back closet. With the mothballs you put in them, I doubt that they are in much shape to wear. You going to the funeral tomorrow? You can use that spare bedroom until you figure out where you want to live. I don't know what they are going to do about the Pig and Poke now that Frank's dead."

"I'm going to the funeral. I'll iron a fresh uniform out of my sea bag. I'll figure out what I've got in civilian clothes after the funeral tomorrow. For now, I'm going to just sit in here and enjoy this bottle of bourbon."

I sat down at my desk and propped my feet up. My black shoes, with a touch of KIWI cordovan, even after getting knocked around on the train, were still glistened next to the forest-green Marine trousers.

"It sure feels good, Joe, to be home. My .38 still in the safe."

"If that's where you left it."

"Now all I need is a babe in my arms."

Joe smiled. "That won't take long. I told you Delana is still around."

"She's probably madder than hell since I didn't write."

"I don't think so. Want me to call her newspaper and tell her you're here?"

"No, not yet. Today it's Martin Mayfield and bourbon as I soak up this office and what it's like to be back."

Joe was smiling as he went out the door. I nursed the bottle of bourbon for a couple of hours amid my thoughts and then went out for a steak dinner. Joe didn't even object when I took the keys off the rack for a gray '50 Ford 2-door. His only comment was, "You still know how to drive?"

"If I don't, your car will be the first to know."

I burned rubber onto Colfax and had trouble keeping it under fifty. Damn, it felt good to be home.

Three

The funeral was well-attended. Frank knew a lot of people from his restaurant and motel business. Friends, employees, and acquaintances filled the small chapel with the white wooden cross at the front of it. Not everyone could get into the chapel; some stood on the cement courtyard in front. If Frank had any relatives I never heard of any and no one seemed to fit that role at the funeral, seated in any special place.

Frank's expensive oak and metal casket was at the front of the chapel. The lid remained closed. The funeral parlor knew that showing a guy's face that had been blasted with a shotgun was too grotesque for your average mourner.

Joe and I had arrived early enough to find seats near the front. Joe wore an appropriate black suit, even though he did spoil it by wearing white socks. I was dressed in a fresh Marine-green uniform I had pulled from my sea bag and ironed. I had touched my shoes up, figuring this would be about the last time I would wear my uniform, and I felt I owed it to the Corps to look my best.

The funeral service was a nondenominational thing, with a minister in a black suit mumbling platitudes about the afterlife. He also said some general things about what a wonderful guy Frank had been. It was my impression that he hadn't known Frank at all, not that Frank hadn't been a wonderful guy, but the minister gave no specifics of Frank's life, other than that he had been the owner of the Pig and Poke. He did not even have Frank's date of birth and it was not printed on the white memorial card they gave each of the mourners.

Sitting two rows in front of us was a nun in a black habit. I assumed she was probably elderly because of the way she bent forward. I couldn't see her face, but I doubted it would look nearly as pretty as the face of the 'nun' I had met on the train.

My mind wandered from the droning words of the minister, who was giving a sermon about the Good Shepherd gathering his flock. I didn't mean to be sacrilegious, but I kept thinking about the naked body of 'Sister Brochetti' when we had been together in the rocking motion of the train.

Six pallbearers, middle-aged to elderly, lifted the casket and took it out the side of the chapel to the black Cadillac hearse. I recognized one of the pallbearers as being from Frank's Rotary Club. My skills as a private detective hadn't been lost during the Korean War and I was pleased that I could remember the face.

A face that I was surprised to see was that of Fat Georgie. As we spilled out of the chapel into the bright late-September sun, bright and clear as it can only be on a Colorado fall day that would push the temperature up close to 80, Fat Georgie's face looked less-than-angelic behind his sunglasses. Two of his torpedoes were with him. Black suits, white silk ties, and dark-gray dress hats, the three of them had 'mob' written all over them. The Marine Corps had its dress code. The mob had its dress code, and apparently black suits, dark-gray hats, white silk ties, and dark sunglasses were in this year.

As Joe and I passed by him, Fat Georgie recognized me. I could tell by the expression on his face. He didn't say anything and neither did I. We hardly shared a mutual affection for each other. Our last meeting, three and a half years before, had been less-than-pleasant. Fat Georgie had warned me to stay out of his territory in North Denver and I had told him I was going to kick the shit out of him when I nailed him for something big someday. I think we had parted with a mutual "kiss my ass" or words to that effect.

I had driven a black 1950 Buick Super convertible 2-door with white side walls to the funeral. Joe had insisted on taking something "dignified", no Ford or Chevies. I had talked him into the convertible after I had spotted it on the lot. Buicks were big and heavy with a grill that reminded me of a toothy smile. The Dynaflow Drive automatic transmission was smooth, but less-than-startling in its acceleration. I liked the comfortable, solid ride, but preferred something with a faster getaway.

As we followed in the long line of cars going into Crown Hill, it seemed much too nice of a day for a funeral. At a little after eleven in the morning, sun was streaming down on trees that were turning fall golden. Maples, Dutch elms, and cottonwoods were spaced throughout the green-lawn cemetery, along with the more numerous pine and spruce that would stay green all year. We drove with the top down and the beautiful day gave me a mood of complete tranquility.

"Frank would have liked this," Joe said.

"Yeh," I grunted. "Did you know he liked to play checkers?"

"Sure. I even joined that checkers club with him while you were away. Bunch of middle-aged guys sitting around playing checkers every Thursday night. It's O.K., but nothing to blow your horn about. Frank acted like it was the highlight of his life."

As the cars made a turn at one of the cemetery intersections I saw the nun sitting in the Yellow Cab. Fat Georgie's '53 black Cadillac 4-door was behind it. We were about ten cars behind them. The mob always seemed to go for 4-door black Cadillacs. Fat Georgie was sitting in the back seat and his two torpedoes were in the front. My curiosity was aroused. Why was Fat Georgie at the funeral? Who was the nun? Was it just coincidental that Fat Georgie's car was behind the nun's taxi?

As we stopped along the side of the narrow, black-asphalt road, a long line of cars extended up to the hearse where they were unloading the coffin. I decided to make it a point to see the nun's face and see if Fat Georgie was either tailing her or guarding her. Joe had a hard time keeping up with me as I moved ahead.

"Jeez, Marty, you're not in the Marines anymore. Go easy on an old guy, will you?"

"Stay back, Joe; there's something I want to see up ahead." I walked even faster, passing mourners and shortening the distance between Fat Georgie and his torpedoes, who were sticking close to the nun. She was walking across the green grass at the normal rate of speed toward the open grave.

As the mourners gathered, I worked my way around the standing crowd to where I was opposite the nun and Fat Georgie. The nun was still keeping her head bent forward, so it was hard to get a good look at her, even though she stood at the front of the crowd.

After the words were spoken, the casket was lowered. The nun knelt and crossed herself, her head bowed, as if in prayer. While still kneeling, she raised her face and I saw her tears. It was 'Sister Brochetti'.

The crowd started to melt away and I tried to close the distance between 'Sister Brochetti' and myself. It was a tough swim, getting through the densely packed crowd, and I didn't make much progress until we were well on our way to the cars.

'Sister Brochetti' was almost to the cab when Fat Georgie's torpedoes grabbed her. I was about twenty feet back and the crowd had thinned enough that I had a running shot at stopping Fat Georgie's torpedoes from throwing her into the back of their Cadillac. She was struggling with the two muscle boys, but they had a handkerchief over her mouth and were pretty much lifting her off her feet as they dragged her the seven or eight feet to the Cadillac.

They were shoving her into the back seat when I slammed into the torpedo on the left, hitting him in the middle of the back with a right shoulder block that bent him back in so much screaming pain that I thought I had broken his back. The other torpedo finished forcing 'Sister Brochetti' into the back seat as I pulled him loose from her and threw him away from the car. His hat and sunglasses flew away from him as he went down.

He came off the ground reaching for his pistol. I kicked him in the face. The force of my foot knocked him backwards and to the side before he slumped face-forward to the ground.

Fat Georgie caught me a glancing blow with a pistol butt on the back of my head as I spun toward him. The blow threw me off balance into the side of the Cadillac and as I regained my balance he turned the barrel of the pistol toward me.

Before he could fire, I lunged, grabbed his wrist with my

left hand and swung his arm away from me. I brought my right arm up under his armpit, cupped my right hand onto his wrist below my left hand and with a shift of body weight, threw him over my right hip. The pistol fell from his hand as he was going down hard. It was ordinary hand-to-hand Marine combat. I had to hold myself in check to keep from killing him.

I let him stagger to his feet. He had lost his hat, and his sunglasses were at an angle on his forehand. The left lens was jaggedly-broken. I shoved him up against the Cadillac.

One of the torpedoes was still unconscious and face down. The one, whose back I thought I might have broken, was hanging onto the Caddie tailfin, standing on wobbly legs, but nevertheless, standing, which told me I hadn't broken his back. He had lost his hat, but his sunglasses were still on.

"Fat Georgie, you're going to make me kill you one of these days," I growled at him through clenched teeth. My left forearm was across his throat. "Don't ever pull a rod on me again. You do and you'll end up being a permanent resident of this place. Now, what the hell are you doing abducting nuns?"

"I don't know," he wheezed. "I get my orders."

"Yeh, I guess you do, but what's the mob want with her?"

"I don't know."

I leaned my weight into my forearm, not much, but just enough to let him know I meant business.

"You're choking me," he wheezed as I released a little of the pressure.

"No shit. You're smarter than I gave you credit for. What's the mob want with the nun?"

"I don't know. He's choking me!" The yell was for the benefit of the mourners who had stopped to watch. I looked around at the ten or so faces gathered around. Joe's face was one of them. I took my arm away from Fat Georgie's throat.

"He assaulted me!" Fat Georgie yelled.

"I saw it. It was three on one," an elderly woman, dressed in funeral black, said, "Hit 'em again, Marine, before they come back at you."

That sounded like a pretty good idea to me. I stepped back and fired an overhand right to Fat Georgie's fat jaw. His head thumped back on top of the Cadillac before he slid down the side of the car into unconsciousness.

"Thank you, ma'am," I said to the elderly woman. It was then I remember 'Sister Brochetti'.

"Joe, where's the sister?"

"You mean the nun, Marty? She went out the other side of the car and hightailed it out of here in a Yellow Cab."

I looked around for the Yellow Cab. It was nowhere to be seen.

Joe asked, "You going to call the police and have these guys arrested for kidnaping?"

"Wouldn't do any good," I replied. "Nobody has been kidnaped. It would just be my word against theirs. Come on, Joe. It was just a cemetery brawl. Let's get out of here before these gorillas come back to life and I have to do it all over again."

I may have misinterpreted the look, but I thought the elderly woman looked disappointed that I wouldn't have to do it again. Joe and I ignored the staring spectators as we walked back to the Buick.

As I pulled out and drove away I could see the guy I had kicked getting up off the ground. That was good. I really didn't want a murder rap or manslaughter charge over a funeral fight. I figured Fat Georgie would revive also. He was breathing when I left him, so I figured he would live.

Four

I dropped Joe at the car lot and went downtown to the headquarters of Yellow Cab. I figured the dispatcher could tell me where the taxi had taken 'Sister Brochetti' from the cemetery. The driver had let her out at the corner of Colfax and Broadway.

Colfax and Broadway, if not the exact geographical center of Denver, was the center of Denver as far as being the place where the two major streets of the city intersected. East of Broadway, south of Colfax, was the state capitol. West of Broadway, south of Colfax, was Civic Center and the City and County Building. North of Broadway was the downtown commercial district. South of Colfax, running along

Broadway, was a commercial row and residential areas that extended miles. What all of this meant was that 'Sister Brochetti' could be anywhere.

I could dog my feet around to all of the downtown hotels and see if she had checked into one. That would take hours. I could check out the big three fairly fast, since they were located very close to each other, the Cosmopolitan, the Shirley Savoy, and the Brown Palace. This I did, parking the Buick in the City and County parking lot and then walking.

The desk clerks gave me nothing--no nuns or no one by the name of ' Sister Brochetti'. Blank stares or a shaking head resulted when I tried to describe her.

I thought about the train depot, the bus station, and the airport. They seemed unlikely since she had not been dropped by the taxi at any of them.

I decided to go visit the Rocky Mountain News. Perhaps I would have better luck in locating Delana Dixon. If she wasn't out on a story, I would probably catch her in the newsroom.

The newsroom was its usual flurry of activity, typewriters pecking, telephones ringing, and people rushing about for no apparent reason. Those not so engaged were drinking coffee or carrying on conversations. Delana was at her desk until she saw me.

Rushing to me, she threw her arms around me and kissed me long and hard. I picked her up off the floor as I held her close. She was crying as I set her back down.

"You louse," she said as her eyes went from wide tears to narrow anger. "You inconsiderate louse. Not one letter, telegram, or telephone call." She slapped my face so hard she snapped my head to the side.

Gripping her wrists so that she couldn't hit me again, I said, "I thought you were glad to see me."

"I am." Her eyes slipped back into tears. "Oh, let go of me; I'm not going to hit you again. But in three years you could have at least sent a postcard or something."

She saw that many of those in the newsroom had stopped what they were doing and were watching us. "This is Martin Mayfield," she called. She whispered to me, "What's your rank?

I started to say 'captain' for the hell of it, but changed my mind and gave her my real rank.

She said loudly, "Gunnery sergeant, U.S. Marine Corps. He is home from the war and if anybody calls for me, I won't be at my desk the rest of the afternoon."

"Why don't we take a picture?" a woman suggested. "Might make a good story. You know, returning-war-hero type of thing."

"Did you do anything heroic, Sergeant?" a man's voice called.

"Let's get out of here," I said in a low voice to Delana.

As we started to walk, the same man's voice called, "Too bad you lost the war. We were behind you a hundred percent."

I recognized the voice. It was Jimmy Delong, a smart-ass reporter I hadn't liked before I went to Korea. I liked him even less now that I was back. He had tried to date Delana before I left. I thought of what might have gone on in my absence. I stopped and turned around. I could see Jimmy grinning at me from where he sat on the edge of a desk. He looked just as jerky in his little red bow tie as I remembered him.

Delana gripped my arm and tried to pull me. "Jimmy, shut up!" she yelled.

"I only meant I wanted the sergeant to know we were glad he was home even though our side lost."

"How would you like me to take that dip-shit bow tie of yours and strangle you with it?" I had tried not to make the remark, but by saying something I was controlling my anger enough to keep from attacking him.

"Please, Marty," Delana said and pulled my arm to leave.

As we left the newsroom I heard Jimmy say in a voice that I knew he didn't think I could hear, "He's lucky he didn't attack me. I would have torn him apart."

I heard someone else say, "Oh sure," and there was a laugh.

The bright Colorado sunshine helped me cool down. "Still as big of a jerk as ever, I see. I don't suppose you dated him while I was gone?"

"Of course not. Did you get married while you were gone? I won't ask about girlfriends. Girlfriends are something I can understand. If you got married, I would find that a little hard to take." She said it lightly, but there was enough tension in her voice that I could tell she was serious.

"I told you before I left, women and wars don't mix. That's why I didn't write. If I would have been killed, then you could have gone on with your life as if I had never been."

She stopped and looked at me. "No, I couldn't have. I told you no strings of any kind. You are free to come and go and have whatever friends you choose, as am I. But that doesn't mean that you're not very special to me. I don't think marriage, even if you wanted to get married, would be good for either of us. We are too independent, both of us. I don't want to tame you and make you miserable. But that doesn't mean I don't care about you more than anyone I have ever known."

I looked down at her with her face fully exposed in the bright sunshine. She was still stunningly beautiful. At the age of 33, a few of the lines at the corner of her eyes had started to deepen and the harsh light of the sun exposed them. At the age of 34, after two wars, I was beginning to wear a little myself, so I could be charitable about any tiny flaws in her beauty. Her round, soft brown eyes were as beautiful and clear as ever. Her high cheekbones still gave her a look of elegance. Her radiant black hair had no traces of gray. With her high heels I didn't have to look down very far at her. Five-feet-five, plus two-inch heels, made her about five inches shorter than I. She was in one of her 'working uniforms', a blue suit.

I smiled and said, "I thought you only cared about captains."

"My first husband was an ass, and I hope you don't begin to act like one too."

"I thought he was a nice guy from what you told me about him."

"Well, he was, but in some ways he was an ass. Have you got someplace in mind to go or do you want to continue this conversation here on the sidewalk? Maybe captains do have better manners than sergeants. I'm sure he wouldn't have gone three years without a letter. When we were parted for three weeks he wrote everyday."

"A real Boy Scout," I said. "So, I'm sorry I didn't write. Now that I'm back, maybe it wasn't such a good idea. At the time, it seemed best. I apologize, O.K.?"

She nodded.

"I've got one of Joe's cars. Let's take a ride up into the mountains. How about an early supper, or late lunch, whichever you prefer at The Ranch? It is still up by Floyd Hill?"

"Still there, and I accept."

The ride into the mountains was beautiful. With the top down, you could almost touch the green pine and spruce trees. Most of the aspen were further up in the mountains, but those we saw on the way up to the restaurant were beginning to wear their beautiful golden fall color. The stench of the Korean War was far away, and I was sorry as we drove up that I hadn't yet had time to get civilian clothes together so that I could retire my uniform. What made it worth wearing was Delana's comment as we ate trout dinners at The Ranch.

"I'm glad you are wearing your uniform, Marty. I've never seen you in a uniform before. You look very handsome."

"Handsome as a captain?"

"He was handsome too, but you are ruggedly handsome. With those ribbons and medals on your chest, I can tell you weren't a desk soldier."

"Marine, Delana. A Marine never likes to be called a soldier. You might say I didn't spend much time behind a desk."

"Want to talk about it, Marty?"

"No."

"I'm proud of you, Marty."

I looked away and out the plate glass window to where I could see pine trees.

"Even though we didn't win and we didn't lose."

"Win, lose, or draw, I'm proud of you."

I looked at her. "Thanks, Delana. I appreciate that." I wanted to change the subject. "Report any good stories lately?"

"Oh, a few. You know me; I'm always digging for that Pulitzer Prize."

I laughed. "And I'll damn well bet you get it someday."

We talked about what had been going on of a news nature since I had been gone. It was like being on another planet for three years. I had almost no idea of national or international news other than that Eisenhower had been elected president and the Korean War had ended. I had heard nothing of local news in three years, so Delana did a lot of filling me in as we relaxed with after-dinner drinks before having coffee and heading back down the mountain. I thought it was interesting that the Coliseum had been built. They were also making progress toward getting a new Denver Public Library, although the old one was still in use and it would be quite sometime before the new one was built.

I suppose we were still a 'cow town', but we were getting to be a bigger 'cow town'. There were even some ski areas starting to develop in the mountains. Guys who had trained in Colorado as Army ski troops in World War II had come back after the war and had built their passion for skiing into blossoming ski runs. I had heard they hadn't done too bad in the war either, kicking the hell out of the Germans in the Italian Alps.

When the subject turned to Frank Brodrick's murder, Delana could tell me little that I hadn't heard from Joe. She did supply one new important bit of information.

"Harry Makris suspects organized crime is involved."

"That would explain Fat Georgie's attendance at the funeral this morning."

"Who is Fat Georgie?"

"A local mob figure. We had a little chat this morning. It wasn't very friendly."

Delana looked sternly at me. "Marty, you haven't gotten yourself in trouble with gangsters already, have you?"

"Nah, just a chance meeting at Frank's funeral this morning. They have probably already forgotten that I was there. Since it looks like organized crime might be involved in Frank's murder, would you do a little research on organized crime for me? No field work, just your newspaper sources and whatever you can read on it. I don't want you getting hurt. I need to know more about how they operate and how they got started. It might help me in getting to Frank's killer. I've had a few brushes with the mob in the past, but if it was a mob killing, I'll need to know more about them than I do now. One of the things the Marine Corps taught me was to know your enemy. The more you know about him, the better chance you have of killing him before he kills you."

"I kind of doubted you would want to be a schoolteacher when you came back, but I was hoping you might try something a little less dangerous than being a private detective."

"No strings, remember?"

"Fair enough, but what is in it for me if I do your research?"

"The story when I catch Frank's killer, if I get to him before the cops do, assuming he can be caught."

"What made you say 'he'? It could be a woman, you know."

"Sure, a member of the mob who uses a shotgun. I think it's a safe bet it's a 'he', but if it is a 'she', you will be the first to know if I nail her."

We drove back to Denver and I dropped Delana at the Rocky Mountain News. She told me to come to her apartment in about two hours. That was fine with me. It gave me time to buy two pair of slacks, one blue and one tan, two sports coats, one blue and one tan, and three shirts, two white and one a flaming red. The red sports shirt was for when I wanted to wear something a little wild. I avoided buying ties, since I hated the things anyway, even on my Marine uniform. Whatever other clothing I needed I could drag out of my mothballed storage boxes.

After hanging the uniform in Frank Galliger's back closet, I shaved, showered and put on the new civilian clothes. I chose for my debut into civilian life blue slacks, tan sports coat and red shirt. So, I hadn't bought my clothes at some fancy store around town; I was a simple guy, with simple tastes. The clothes looked fine to me.

"Jeez, Marty, you look different," Joe said as I was leaving the car lot. "I think you looked better in your uniform."

"Thanks. I needed that," I replied sarcastically as I piled into the Buick and pulled away. Even though the fall night air was cool, I left the top down. As I tapped out a Lucky, lit it from the car lighter, and listened to the music on the radio,

I really felt free.

When Delana opened the door, she was in a peach-colored negligee and white high heels. Her body under the negligee looked more-than-enticing.

"You might have been embarrassed if it wasn't me." I said.

"Are you sure?" she asked as she closed the door behind me. She led me into the bedroom.

"When you get time, Marty, I'm going to take you to some decent men's clothing stores."

"You don't like my new clothes?"

"At least not on you. Don't you think it is about time we got to know each other again?" She lightly kissed the bottom of my ear and started unbuttoning my shirt.

"Ah, Montgomery Ward's clothes, they'll do it every time." I said, wasting no time in getting out of my new clothes. My only comment was, "You know you are fabulous, don't you?" She really was.

Five

Harry Makris hadn't changed in any way that I could notice. He was still five-eight, about 150 pounds, dark hair, dark eyes and a complexion that was dark enough to be Southern European. He still wore a dark-gray suit and a gray tie. He didn't look any older, but he was three years older than when I left for the Marines, which made him 35. While he was puzzling something out, he still had the annoying habit of using his thumb and forefinger to stroke his narrow black mustache.

After preliminary greetings at the police station we settled into a drink at a downtown bar. Harry selected this particular bar because it was a place where his captain would be less likely to detect that he was drinking while on duty. Drinking was not strictly forbidden to detectives, but it was discouraged unless it was a productive method of gaining information. Harry drank a bottle of Coors beer while I had a bourbon and water.

"How was it?" Harry asked. "Was it as bad as the last one?"

He didn't have to explain. I knew exactly what he meant. He had been in the Army infantry during World War II, making the invasion at Sicily and slogging his way up the Italian peninsula. He hadn't made it into Rome. His Purple Heart was like mine, only his wound had been in the leg rather than in the back like mine.

"It was as bad. For me the last one was a hot hell of steaming jungles and volcanic rock. This one was a frozen hell of snow and ice, with spring and summer mud. Take your choice, Harry. It's all the same."

"I'm glad I missed it."

We could talk. He had been through it, and he knew what I was talking about. That was one of the bonds that made us good friends; that plus our mutual interest in taking down the bad guys.

After further talk about the wars and his wife and now three kids--he had added one while I was gone--I asked him about Frank's murder. He said he would take time to run me out to the scene of the crime.

"What about your captain?" I asked.

"This is police work. It is one of my cases, so Captain Garret shouldn't have a beef about me visiting the crime scene as many times as I want with anybody I want to take with me. If you haven't lost the touch, you might turn up some useful information for me."

"You mean like the time I had you waiting in a closet with Joe Galliger while we were trying to nail Barry Hampton?"

We both laughed. That episode had become a source of amusement to us. Joe Galliger had never been told why he had been asked to hide in a closet with Harry. He was supposed to become a witness against Barry Hampton. Hampton had thwarted the plan; thus, Joe's testimony was never used, which was fine, since he would have had nothing to testify.

At the new Denver Coliseum Harry gained entrance through a side door and took me into the center of the arena. We looked up into the rows of wooden seats as we stood on the dirt floor.

"I thought you would like to see it from this angle. It kind of gives you the feeling of what it must be like for one of those steers as a cowboy bulldogs him to the ground."

"Harry, do I look like the cowboy type in this blue sports coat and white shirt?"

"Well, the least you could do is wear a tie sometime. Are you sure you're not a cowboy?"

A voice called, ringing in the hollow open pit, "You fellows here to see about the vending jobs?" We shifted around and saw a man standing in one of the cement portals about a fourth of the way up in the circular rows of seats. "Oh, it's you, Detective Makris. I guess you wouldn't be looking for a job then."

"No, but thanks, Dave. Maybe you've got something for my friend here. Need anybody to clean up after the animals or anything?"

"I wouldn't know, Mr. Makris. You would have to talk to the arena manager about that. His office is on the top floor."

"Thanks, Dave."

"Thanks a lot, Harry. You seem to have turned into a real comedian during my absence."

Harry chuckled. "You Marines too tough to laugh once in awhile?"

Harry was one of the few people I would let get away with a remark like that.

"Yeh, I guess you're right; it's time to lighten up a bit. Go ahead, be funny, Harry. I'll laugh. How is your impression of Groucho Marx?"

"Not too good. Come on; I'll show you the tunnel." I followed him from the arena into a round cement tunnel about fifteen-feet-high with a dirt floor. "What was your rank when you got out?"

"Gunnery sergeant. That's the same as your Army tech. sergeant, three up and two down."

"That's pretty good. I only came back as a buck sergeant and that's after getting my ass shot off in Italy."

"But you only had one war to work with. Besides, they don't give higher NCO ranks to comedians."

Harry was through playing around. We were at the scene of the crime and Harry was first and always a good cop.

"There is not much to see. This is where he was standing, and this is where somebody blew his head off. We think the shotgun was a twelve-gage. You see the blood still on the wall. We asked the Stock Show people not to clean it off yet. None of the spectators can see it in here. But that doesn't matter much since they haven't done any shows yet."

"What do they use this tunnel for?" I asked, touching the toe of my shoe into the dirt where Frank was standing when he was shot.

"You aren't a cowboy, Marty. This is how they bring the animals in from the stock pens when they are going to use them or exhibit them in the arena."

"So, an assailant could have entered either way, from the arena the way we came, or from the stock pens?"

"Either way, and I don't see that it makes much difference. When the Coliseum isn't in use, it's accessible to about anyone."

"And Frank could have come in either way also," I said.

"Sure." Harry was playing with his mustache with his left hand, and his right hand was on his hip. "The way I figure it, Frank came here to a meeting of some kind. There were no signs of a struggle in the dirt or signs of anyone dragging somebody here. We got some footprints that the lab has been working on. Two people with size ten shoes, one with a nine, one with a size eleven, and one a size twelve. Frank's shoe size was a twelve, so we figure there were four guys and Frank."

"Assuming the footprints aren't of some of the workers around here."

"Cowboys wear cowboy boots. The guys who work here either wear cowboy boots, work boots, or high-top work shoes. When you are using a pitchfork to move hay, or shoveling up horse or cow manure, you don't wear dress shoes. Boots and work shoes make a decidedly different mark in the dirt. Besides, the Stock Show doesn't hit town until January, so I doubt we have had many workers in here."

"Where was the shooter standing?"

"Whoever used the shotgun was standing about here when he pulled the trigger. It must have made a hell of a noise in this tunnel. He gave Frank both barrels at almost the same time. A double-barreled shotgun at close range can be a very effective weapon. Frank was tall and the blast went up at a slight angle. We figure it was fired from the shoulder with the end of the barrels about five feet from Frank's head. There just wasn't much left of Frank's head."

"They had the coffin closed at the funeral."

"You got home in time for the funeral?"

"Yeh, and I ran into Fat Georgie and a couple of torpedoes there. You got anything on Fat Georgie on this case?"

"Not yet, but I have had him and the rest of the North-Denver mob under consideration. I figure this has all the marking of a professional hit by the mob, whether it was Fat

Georgie or somebody else who did the hitting. So far, I haven't been able to make a direct connection to anybody, but we are working at it."

I went to the cement wall and started examining the bloodstains on it. There were pits in the cement from the buckshot. I thought my examination of the wall wouldn't show me anything, but I was in the habit of examining as much as I could at the scene of the crime. I continued to examine as I spoke.

"After I saw Fat Georgie at the funeral I asked Delana to do some research for me on organized crime, to find out more about how they operate. You knew Frank tipped me on how to get to Irene Hampton's killers in the mob on that case. I figure Frank had to know somebody in the mob or something. He piped me into them all the way into New York. Is our local mob tied in with the New York mob?"

"They had some Congressional hearings on crime while you were away. Did you hear about them, the Kefauver hearings?"

I turned away from the wall. I was tired of looking at the bloodstains and the pits. "No." I heard something about Joe McCarthy and some hearings on communism, but I don't know much about them or, what was the guy you mentioned?"

"Senator Estes Kefauver. He showboated on television for awhile, had practically the whole country watching. There has been a lot of attention focused on organized crime lately."

"One thing I've noticed since I got back is all the TV sets. I hardly saw a TV set before I left. Now TV is all over town. Joe Galliger has even got one in his car lot office. Well, anyway, I thought Thomas Dewey cleaned up organized crime in New York in the 1930's. That was supposed to be the end of it."

"That's what Dewey thought. As you recall, his

reputation for being tough on crime almost got him elected president. He couldn't beat F.D.R. in 1944 or Truman in 1948, but he was one of the best investigators and prosecutors this country has ever had. He put a dent in New York City crime, but if you don't keep after it, crime comes back like a weed. Lately, we've been hearing something about the possibility of a nationwide crime organization, with New York City being its headquarters. It's called the MAFIA or something like that, and it's run by Italians. I guess it has some Jews. You remember Bugsy Siegal?"

"He got blown away out in California after opening the Flamingo in Las Vegas. I think it was 1947."

"That was a crime hit. We figure he was a part of organized crime. Siegal was Jewish, but we figure most of it is run by Italians. We can't finger it, but the Federal Bureau of Narcotics has been running off about this MAFIA or whatever they call it. The rest of us are beginning to believe that the narcotics boys know what they are talking about."

"So, you think our North-Denver mob might be a part of it?"

"Seems very possible. It makes me madder than hell because of what it does to the rest of us Italians, makes us look like criminals."

"I thought you were Greek."

"My father is Greek. My mother is Italian."

"You are mixed up," I said, trying to show Harry that I still had a sense of humor. "How will you ever know what you are?"

"I know what I am, an American, but I'm proud of my Greek and Italian heritage. So, what are you, smart-ass?"

"American mongrel. English, German, Irish, and Indian, as nearly as I can figure it."

Harry went on, "Most Italians are law-abiding good American citizens, as are Jews. You go out along West Colfax before you get to Marty's car lot and you'll find Jews in synagogues, living hard-working, law-abiding lives. You go north from Colfax and you'll find Italians praying in their Catholic churches and living hard-working, law-abiding lives. Just like Irish cops, some are on the take, but most are law-abiding, good Americans. I want to nail Frank's killers, especially if they turn out to be Italian. I want to show that an Italian cop can take down Italians."

"You're Greek, Harry."

"Only if I want to be. Right now I'm Italian mad. That's my interest in this case, other than the professional interest the taxpayers pay me for. I knew Frank was your friend and landlord. Any other interest?"

"Eighteen-hundred bucks."

"Why, somebody hire you?"

"While I was away I sent Frank fifty bucks a month so that I would have some money when I came home. Run across it in your investigation?"

"Everything that Frank had is on hold while they figure out if Frank had any relatives or left a will. I suppose probate court has jurisdiction. Somebody dies suddenly, no apparent heirs, it takes awhile to sort things out."

"What happens to his business in the meantime?"

"His employees are running it, but that is only temporary. The court may padlock it if they don't figure out who owns it soon. As of now, no one but Frank's heirs, in the absence of a will, has a legal right to operate it. Rather than throw everyone out of a job who is working there and evict whoever is living at the motel, the law will look the other way for a few days while looking for heirs or a will. Are you living at the Pig and Poke now?"

"I've been staying with Joe Galliger until I figure out where I want to live. I may go to the Pig and Poke or I may go elsewhere. Then again, I may just stay with Joe for awhile."

"Why don't you marry Delana? That would solve your

problem of where to live."

"Harry, you snoop too much."

Harry laughed. "Come on, Marty; let's get out of this tunnel. You hungry yet? It's almost noon."

I followed him, feeling like a cow being led to the slaughter. "Not that Greek restaurant. I still don't like all that lamb and stuff."

"You will like this. It's something we have started getting in Denver. I'm an Italian, remember? We're going to North Denver. On 38th they've got one of the best pizza parlors in town."

"Pizza, what's that?"

"It's something they brought in from back east. Italians had it in New York or Chicago or something; now Denver Italians have it."

"What if we run into Fat Georgie or some of the mob?"

"We won't. They still hang out at Vitaliano's Restaurant and Lounge. That is something that hasn't changed since you have been gone. Where we are going we are more likely to run into high school kids. And it's not just the Italian kids that like it; all kids really dig this pizza stuff."

"Are you young at heart, Harry?"

"When I'm an Italian, yes."

We squeezed into the pizza parlor with the crowd of kids who had come from North High on their lunch hour. I watched the kids string long strands of cheese out as they ate. I couldn't avoid stringing the cheese out either as we ate the hot, thick crust with the sausage that had been put on top of it.

Harry and the kids were right about the pizza. It was really good, and I thought it wouldn't take long for it to catch on in Denver with the adults too. I could foresee the day when pizza might be as popular as good old American hot dogs or hamburgers, which I figured were probably of German origin. In the Marines, before shipping out for

Korea, a Mexican friend of mine, Sergeant Leroy Sandoval, had introduced me to something else I thought was pretty good.

"Anyplace we can get tacos?" I asked Harry as we left the pizza parlor.

"You mean that Mexican stuff?"

I just thought since we were being ethnic, we might think about tacos the next time we eat together."

"I give you good Italian pizza, and you bring up some Mexican food nobody has ever heard of."

"The Mexicans have, Harry. I tried them when I was in California. They're really good. You ought to try them sometime."

"Well, maybe." Harry frowned. "The next time I work with Joe Gallegos, I'll ask him about them. I'm not trying anything until I know what it is."

"Very enlightened, Harry. I'm glad I felt that way about pizza."

We got into Harry's unmarked black '51 Ford.

"Think we can get Dean Martin on the radio?" I asked.

"We only listen to police stuff when we are in the car."

"How come a good Italian singer and performer like Dean Martin has a name like Dean Martin? He is Italian, isn't he?"

"Dino Crocetti."

"What?"

"Dino Crocetti. That was his real name. His stage name, Marty, is Dean Martin."

"Oh. How about Frank Sinatra and Perry Como?"

"I wouldn't know. As far as I know, those are their real names."

"Do Italians sing a lot, Harry?"

"That's the last time I'm taking you to an Italian joint."

"You can skip the Greek places too."

I think Harry was happy to end the conversation by looking over his shoulder as he pulled away from the curb.

Six

"Harry, there is something I ought to tell you," I said as we headed toward Federal Boulevard. "When I saw Fat Georgie and his torpedoes at the funeral, I roughed them up a bit. They were trying to snatch some nun and I stopped them."

"You mean 'snatched', as in 'kidnaped'?"

"You got it."

"Who is she?"

"I don't know. She got away from them and me. Run a check on a Sister Brochetti. I heard that name."

"How bad did you rough up Fat Georgie and his torpedoes?"

"I left two of them unconscious and one of them thinking he had a broken back, which he didn't."

Harry pulled the car to the side of the street and stopped. "Marty, you're here two days and already you've got the mob mad enough to rub you out. They don't take kindly to having somebody mug their boys."

"It was either that or let them shove this nun into their car at Crown Hill. I stopped them and by the time I got through with them, she had left. Joe Galliger said she left in the Yellow Cab that brought her to the cemetery."

"Maybe I can trace her through the cab company."

"I already did. The cab dropped her at Broadway and Colfax. I checked a few downtown hotels but I couldn't find any trace of her."

"Any idea why the mob wanted her?"

"None. I just saw then trying to grab her at the cemetery, so I stopped them."

Harry fingered his mustache while he thought. Then he asked, "You carrying a piece?"

"I've got my .38. I haven't renewed my permit since I got home, so I don't know if I'm legal."

"Keep it in your holster unless I really need it. We are going to make a call to Vitaliano's Restaurant and Lounge. I haven't got anything on them since we haven't got a kidnap victim to make a complaint, but, at least, I can let them know you've got police protection. Maybe that will keep them from blowing your head off."

Harry called on the radio for a black and white back-up, giving instructions that it was to meet us at Vitaliano's Restaurant and Lounge. By way of explanation he told me as he pulled away from the curb, "I suppose visiting these guys is a dumb thing to do, but I'm not dumb enough to go in there without being able to call for help if we really need it."

Harry parked across the street from Vitaliano's in a no-parking truck-loading zone in front of a warehouse. We waited a few minutes for the black and white before going in. When the black and white parked behind us, Harry stepped back and said a few words to the two officers. Then Harry and I went across the street and entered the restaurant part of Vitaliano's. A hostess, an attractive woman in her twenties, greeted us and asked if we wanted the restaurant or the lounge.

Harry looked around the restaurant tables and said, "Lounge."

"It is through the curtains at the back, sir."

We walked through the tables that were filled with a large lunch-time crowd. People came for the good food and some of them came for the thrill of eating at a known-gangster gathering place. It was kind of sheik for some of the city's business types, figuring they were perfectly safe as daytime patrons.

As we started through the hanging multicolored bead strings that formed a curtain, a gorilla, that looked like he was about 300 pounds, stopped us. His voice was amazingly polite-sounding. "You gentlemen here for drinks?"

"Police," Harry replied. "If you want to see my badge, I'll reach inside my coat for it. I just want you to know so you won't think I'm reaching for my revolver."

The gorilla came off the high bar stool that was placed by the door. His demeanor changed for the worse. "Beat it."

"I want to see Sam Vitaliano," Harry replied calmly.

"He ain't here."

"Then maybe we'll just look around for him."

The gorilla placed an arm across Harry's chest. "You got a search warrant?"

"I don't need it, Harry continued in the same calm voice. "This is a public place. We can either do this the easy way or the hard way. You look out the front door and you will see a police car with two officers in it. You can have cops crawling all over the place, disrupting your lunch-time crowd, or you can tell Sam Vitaliano I want to see him."

"Wait here," he said, using his polite voice again. "I'll tell Mr. Vitaliano you're here. Who should I say is calling?"

"Detective Makris and Mayfield." I noticed Harry threw my name in with his, figuring the door guard would associate me with 'detective' also, even though I wasn't dressed like Harry.

The door guard went through an old-style, wooden, saloon swinging doors and returned a couple of minutes later with two torpedoes. In the meantime, Harry and I had been observing the bar crowd, which was like the usual bar crowd. The place was about three-fourth's full. The patrons were almost exclusively male.

"These gentlemen will show you into Mr. Vitaliano's presence."

One of the torpedoes nodded toward the saloon doors. He was obviously holding a rod in his right suit-coat pocket, as was his buddy.

"Thank you," I said to the door guard. What the hell, he was being polite. My seventh-grade teacher had taught me that an extended courtesy should be reciprocated.

Harry followed one of the torpedoes by the bar and through the wooden saloon doors, with me right behind him and the other torpedo behind me. Sam Vitaliano was holding lunch-time court at a long table. There were two empty seats at the end opposite Vitaliano, presumable belonging to the two guys who had ushered us into Vitaliano's presence. Among Vitaliano's twelve disciples were Fat Georgie and the two torpedoes I had roughed up at the cemetery. Fat Georgie and the one I had kicked had swollen, bruised faces. The other one was sitting with a very stiff back.

Vitaliano was a man in his sixties, round of face, nearly bald except for a little gray hair on the sides, a few long strands of which he had combed across the top of his baldhead. He reminded me a little of a cue ball with string on top of it. His dark eyes were not matched by dark circles under them. Apparently, Sam Vitaliano slept quite well at night and did not drive himself excessively hard.

Vitaliano's lunch guests had finished eating, and mostly empty plates sat in front of them as they smoked and drank coffee or wine. Fat Georgie and the two torpedoes I had roughed up showed no recognition of me, although I was sure they were well aware of who I was.

"Detective Makris," Vitaliano said in a voice that denoted neither anger nor alarm, "what is it you and your associate wish to see me about?"

Harry replied equally civilly, "Three of your associates tried to abduct a nun at Frank Brodrick's funeral yesterday. This is the gentleman who prevented the nun from being kidnaped. He was merely acting as a good citizen who saw someone forcefully seizing a nun and acted to stop it. That is what most of us would do if we saw somebody bothering a holy sister. What I would like to know is why were some of your associates attempting to kidnap a nun?"

Although Harry had not used my name, Vitaliano had no trouble finding it when he answered. "Mr. Mayfield was mistaken in what he saw. My associates were merely assisting an elderly nun into her cab. She left the cemetery unharmed. Perhaps Sergeant Mayfield, having just returned from military service, was a bit hasty in his assessment of what was transpiring. Cemeteries are not battlefields, unless we choose to make them so."

"Let's cut the shit, Vitaliano," I said, in a less-polite tone than had been in use. "Fat Georgie and the two torpedoes sitting on each side of him tried to snatch a nun. I saw it; it happened; and no amount of bullshit is going to alter that fact. What were your boys doing picking up a nun at Frank Brodrick's's funeral?"

Some of the guys at the table bristled at my remark, but none of them reached for their rods. I figured the torpedoes behind us still had their rods and could drill us before either of us moved. Sam Vitaliano showed no emotion other than a narrowing of his eyes.

Harry put his arm in front of me as if restraining me or protecting me and quickly said, "What Mr. Mayfield means is that we have sufficient reason to believe that the good sister was forcibly being placed into the automobile of your associates. It is obvious that we do not have the sister or appropriate charges would be filed. But if any harm comes to the sister or Mr. Mayfield, arrests will be made and charges will be filed."

Sam Vitaliano's voice was still civil as he replied, "Mr. Mayfield is fortunate that you are obviously a man of good manners. Coming to my dining table and saying ugly words is not how we do business. I have many police friends and you could become one of them."

"Not a chance," Harry replied. "I'm a cop, doing my job, which is questioning you about the incident with the nun. It is also my responsibility to protect Mr. Mayfield, which I and the police department will do. My concern in this matter is that neither the nun nor Mr. Mayfield comes to any harm. I appreciate a civil discussion when there is no need to resort to unpleasant words or actions. Consider yourself warned about the nun and Mr. Mayfield. I will talk to Mr. Mayfield about his manners."

"Shit," I said in disgust, "I thought you were a tough cop, Harry. What the hell are you doing inflating these guys' ego?"

"I am a tough cop," Harry said. "This is the way we Italians do business in North Denver. Let's go. Our business here is finished. Mr. Vitaliano and I understand each other."

"You are Italian?" Vitaliano asked. "How is it your name is Makris? That doesn't sound Italian."

"My father is Greek. My mother is Italian. I'm Italian when I want to be or Greek when I want to be."

"If you become more Italian than Greek, maybe you should talk to me sometime."

"I'm always American, so I won't be talking to you. Thank you for your time, Mr. Vitaliano. I hope I won't have to be contacting you again in regard to the nun or Mr. Mayfield. The next time it may not be pleasant for either of us."

Harry turned, hesitating to make sure I would follow him. Before I turned I said, "How is your chin, Fat Georgie? I'm sorry I may have bruised it. Perhaps next time we can hold hands and play ring around the tombstone."

Fat Georgie started to reach for his piece in his shoulder holster. A look from Sam Vitaliano restrained him. Harry pulled on my arm.

"I was just trying to be polite," I said to Harry as we started to walk away, making the remark loud enough that Sam Vitaliano and his torpedoes could hear me. "You and Mr. Vitaliano said I should learn to be polite."

"Polite, not stupid," Harry said. We went through the wooden saloon doors.

As we started through the bead curtains separating the bar and the restaurant I said, "Thank you. We had a most enjoyable time."

The door guard looked a little puzzled and then said, "You're welcome."

After Harry had sent the black and white in its way and we piled back into the unmarked black Ford, we both started to talk at the same time. We were both mad, but over different things. I managed to get the first uninterrupted question in.

"What the hell are you doing playing patty cake with those guys."

"What the hell are you doing trying to get us killed?"

"Shit, they weren't going to pop us there."

"No, well how about elsewhere? I don't plan on getting

my head blown off when there is no good reason for it. Besides, you use profanity when there is no call to do so. He got the message."

"What message is that, that you are a cop who plays patty cake?"

"No, that I'm a cop who can't be bought and that he had better lay off the nun and you or I'll nail him."

"I guess you did let him know pretty clearly that you can't be bought. Where did he get the idea you could?"

This time it was Harry's turn to use profanity, which he usually only did when he was emphasizing something very strongly. "Shit, Marty, how do you think those guys operate? They bribe cops. They bribe politicians. Without the support of cops and government leaders they couldn't operate. We'd nail them out of existence. I don't know who on the force is taking bribes, and I don't want to know. I don't know who is taking kickbacks at City Hall and I don't want to know. I do know there are numbers and slots being run in this town, and prostitution. But I don't want to know because I don't want to get my head blown off."

"Does that mean you look the other way?"

"Hell no, I don't look the other way. It just means I don't poke around on things that don't concern me. If it comes up, I deal with it. If we can nail those guys for Frank Brodrick's murder or anything else, I'll do it. But I'm not leaning on the mob until I've got something solid."

"How about nailing Sam Vitaliano for trying to bribe you?"

"He invited me to be his friend and talk to him. I know what he meant, but you think that would stand up in court?"

"How come you were so damn polite to them?"

"That's the code. They don't take out honest cops who are just doing their job. If I get in the way or lean too hard, that could change. They look at it as doing business. They have their business to do and I have my business to do."

Harry started the car and we pulled away from the curb.

"So, do you think I'm in their way enough that they will try to take me out?"

"Not at this point. That's why I let them know you were just a good citizen protecting a nun. You nose around too much in Frank Brodrick's murder and get too close to them and that will change. Let me handle the police work and you're safe. You get in the way and they'll try to take you out. So, stay out of it and let me try nail them."

"You know I won't do that."

Harry glanced at me in exasperation. "Shit, I know that, Marty. But, damn it, use your head instead of your brawn."

"I think they are guilty of Frank's murder. You think that, Harry?"

"Hell yes. But nailing them is the damn problem."

"Harry, you're swearing too much."

Harry smiled. "I guess you are right. I don't want to take this home to my wife and kids. When are you going to come over to see the little guy? He's two now."

"What did you name him?"

"Martin Harry Makris."

"Thanks, Harry," I said. "That makes me very proud."

"What makes you think I named him after you? Maybe it was some guy I busted."

I felt a little overawed at having somebody named after me. I said, "I really appreciate it."

"The oldest one is named Harry Jr. The second is a girl. I guess I just ran out of names. Maybe I was just feeling patriotic about you being away in Korea."

"Can we go see him now, Harry?"

"In case you haven't noticed, I'm on duty. I'll have you over for dinner in a day or two. Charlene likes me to let her know before I bring people home for dinner. That's one of the little things you will learn if you ever get married."

I didn't reply. I was thinking of what an honor it was to

have somebody named after me.

Seven

I put in a long-distance call to the Little Sisters of Charity in Los Angeles. I talked to the Mother Superior and she had no recollection of a 'Sister Brochetti' ever having been a part of the order. She further stated that no members of the order had recently left Los Angeles to attend a funeral in Denver. That also included girls who were in the girls' school and orphanage run by the order. The Mother Superior explained that the Little Sisters of Charity took in orphans and girls from troubled homes. The order cared for them, schooled them, and reared them with Catholic ideals.

Before hanging up I asked permission to visit the order and look over photographs of members of the order and girls they cared for. The Mother Superior was reluctant to grant permission until I explained that someone calling herself 'Sister Brochetti' was masquerading as a nun from the order. I gained further acceptance of the idea of a visit by giving her the telephone number of the Denver Police Department. I told her to ask for Detective Harry Makris. I said he could vouch for my good intentions and would further explain why we would be interested in learning about 'Sister Brochetti' and why she was masquerading as a member of the order. I told her I would call Detective Makris later to see whether or not she had granted permission for a visit.

The rest of the day I hung around the Pig and Poke and questioned employees. They knew nothing about any difficulties Frank Brodrick may have been having with anyone. Ida, who had been with Frank for eleven years, and was now managing the restaurant and motel in his absence, was still visibly distraught by Frank's death. She occasionally had to dab a Kleenex to her eyes as we sat in a restaurant booth drinking coffee and recalling things about Frank while I was fishing for information. She was about fifty, with dyed reddish-yellow hair. The tears didn't improve her narrow face with deep lines.

"I can't imagine who would want to kill him," Ida said repeatedly.

The most interesting thing I got out of her was that Frank had taken a mysterious trip about a year earlier. What was unusual about it was that Frank was gone for over three weeks. Frank would not tell her anything other than he was going to be out of town for a little while. Except for this one time he always provided her with a telephone number where he could be reached in case of problems or questions concerning the restaurant and motel. He had always given her a definite time when he would return, except in this one instance.

"Where did he go on the other trips? Did he give you any

information on where he would be?"

"Just a little general information. I always knew he would be in Los Angeles. That is the only place he ever went."

"Where in Los Angeles?"

"He never said. All he did was leave a telephone number. It was always the same number."

"Do you still have the number?"

"Yes, I'll get it for you."

"Not yet. In a minute. How frequently did he go to L.A.?"

"He went three times a year, the first week in April, the first week in July, and the fourth week in December. He was always gone exactly nine days."

"And he never told you what he did on those trips or anything about them?"

"Never."

"Did he have any particular reaction or mood when he took the usual trips to L.A. or the unusual trip that lasted for over three weeks? Did he react differently or have a different mood in regard to the unusual trip?"

Ida thought a minute before answering.

"Yes, I would say he was much more tense before and after that long trip than he was on his normal trips. He seemed to be watching something for about a month or so. Then he seemed to go back to normal."

"Could he have been watching for somebody to try to do him bodily harm?"

"Very possible. Frank never seemed to be afraid of anything, but he sure kept an eye out for who was coming into the restaurant."

"More than usual when he came back from the unusual trip?"

"More than usual."

Ida got me the telephone number. I had the long-distance

operator call it. There was no answer. I asked the long-distance operator for a listing of the number. It was listed in the name of Frank Brodrick at a West Franklin Street address in Los Angeles. Why had Frank had a listed residence in L.A.? I figured I would check it out when I went to L.A. to visit the Mother Superior at the Little Sisters of Charity.

I decided on a visit to Frank's checkers club before making the trip to L.A. The club only met every Thursday night, and since it was Thursday, I would avail myself of the opportunity before I left for L.A. in the morning. I was going to L.A. whether or not the Mother Superior gave me permission to visit the Little Sisters of Charity, which I assumed she would. I needed to check out Frank's L.A. address, and I was, one way or the other, going to find out if 'Sister Brochetti' had any association with the Little Sisters of Charity.

The checkers club met in a recreation hall next to the swimming lockers and change room at Berkeley Park. The lake had been open in years past for summer-time swimming, with a pier and lifeguard towers. Swimming in city lakes had been in limbo for several years as the city re-evaluated its policy of keeping city lakes open for public swimming in the summer. There was a question about public health and safety, particularly when polio epidemics struck; thereby, causing the posting of signs 'CLOSED: POLIO OUTBREAK'. Since we were moving into the month of October, the lake would have been closed to swimming for the year anyway, but the question of how to use the facility for other-than-swimming purposes was being decided in favor of recreation. It had been used the last couple of years as a checkers club on Thursday nights, with other recreational pursuits taking place on other nights.

About thirty guys, mostly middle-aged or older, were hunched over checkerboards or standing, waiting for games, as I entered the room. There were long green picnic tables and benches spread around the room with clusters of checkers players gathered in no set pattern at the tables and benches. Joe Galliger was not with me because he really didn't care that much for checkers, but he had given me instructions on when and where the club met.

An elderly little guy, with pinch-nose glasses and white hair, sat behind a counter near the entrance. The counter had been used to give out towels when the lake was open to swimming. He asked me, "You here to play checkers or join the club?"

"I don't know. I thought I would see what it is like. Mind if I watch some games?"

"Help yourself. How did you hear about us?"

"I was a friend of Frank Brodrick. He invited me here when he was alive. Now that he is gone, I guess I feel guilty about never taking him up on it."

"Terrible, terrible thing about Frank. One of our best members."

"Who did Frank usually play checkers with? He sure seemed to like the club."

"Oh, he played with everybody, as we all do. I suppose his best friends were Paulie Lovatto and Carlo Lambini. They seemed to like each other's company and played together a lot."

"Maybe I'll watch their games. It might help me to get into it. I've never played much checkers. Are they here?"

"We play some pretty sharp games," he said while peering at me through the top part of his eyeglasses. We don't mind amateurs if they are willing to learn. Are you willing to learn?"

"I'm willing to try, but that's why I think I ought to watch first. I wouldn't want to get into competition over my head."

"Well, Lovatto and Lambini are good, but not our best, so I suppose they would be good to observe. They are about the middle of our skill level, so you can judge for yourself. They are playing each other right now, over at the table in the corner." He pointed to two guys in their late fifties, about the same age as Frank had been. The thin one had pepper-gray hair combed straight back and a thin pepper-gray mustache. The heavy-set one was almost bald. I wondered if fat guys did go bald faster than other guys or if it just seemed that way.

"Thanks," I said.

I walked over and stood by the picnic table where they were playing. Two other guys were playing at the opposite end of table.

"Mind if I watch?" I asked.

"Help yourself," the heavy-set guy grunted as he looked quickly at me and then went back to concentrating on the game that looked as if it was just about over. One player was down to two red kings and no individual checkers. The other player had three black kings and two individual checkers that had almost reached king status.

"I was a friend of Frank Brodrick." I said as I sat down on the bench and reached into my shirt pocket for my pack of Luckies.

The game stopped immediately and they looked at me.

"Which one of you is Lovatto and which one is Lambini?" I asked, tapping a Lucky out of the pack and then offering them the pack, which they declined.

"What's it to you?" the thin one with the mustache asked.

"As I said, I was a friend of Frank Brodrick. He mentioned you guys as his friends. I'm just trying to figure out what happened to him. I come home from the Marines and he's dead. The cops tell me he got his head blown off, but they don't know why. I knew he played checkers with you guys every Thursday night. I just wanted to know if you had heard anything about why somebody would want to kill him. He was a hell of a good guy."

I lit the Lucky with my Marine Corps lighter and waited

for them to answer.

"We ain't heard nothin'," the thin one said.

The fat guy asked, "You Marty Mayfield?"

"The same," I replied.

"Frank used to tell us about you," the fat guy continued. "He even told us about you getting a Cadillac once."

"That's enough, Paulie," the thin guy said in a voice that became razor-sharp.

"Oh, you're Carlo then. Frank said you were an O.K. guy; how come you don't want Paulie to talk to me?"

"He can talk, but it's just that we don't know nothin'."

"Nothing about what?"

"Nothin' about nothin'."

"O.K.," I said. "I didn't come to make you mad. I came to see a couple of Frank's good friends and I thought you would be my friends too. I'm sorry if I upset you. Go on with your game and I'll keep my mouth shut."

Paulie Lovatto stuck out his hand. "I'll be your friend, Mayfield. I'm sorry Frank is dead and I hope whoever did it gets the same."

"My sentiments exactly," I agreed as I shook his hand. I saw Carlo Lambini scowl. "O.K., Mayfield, you can be our friend, but we don't know nothin'. But the one thing I do know is that you are rubbing some people the wrong way here on the north side. I heard through the grapevine you better go easy. Things on this side of town may be a little different than in other parts of town, if you catch my meaning?"

"Then you do know something," I pressed.

"Nothing! Not a damn thing!" Lambini said it so loud that the players at the other end of the table stopped and looked at us. They resumed their game when he went on in a calmer voice, "We are here to play checkers. You can watch, play, or leave."

"I'll leave," I said, deciding that making them angry was not the way to pump them for information. I knew they knew things about Frank's death that they weren't telling me, but it would keep until I got back from L.A. The next time I saw them, they might be friendlier if we parted on good terms. "I'm sorry if I seem a little nosey. I figure I owe it to Frank to find out what I can."

"You in the private detective business again?" Lovatto asked. His voice sounded approving.

"I guess, if I can get any cases. Here are a couple of my business cards." I had taken the cards out of my desk. The telephone number was the number of Joe Galliger's Car Lot. I had my own telephone number in my office, but since I was rarely there and I had never become prosperous enough to hire a secretary, it made sense to use Galliger's business number. "Ask for me at Joe Galliger's Car Lot if I can be of any help to you or you think of anything in connection with Frank's death."

"We won't," Lambini said. Seeing Lovatto's face, I wasn't sure about that.

"Nice to have met you," Lovatto said as I took a drag on the Lucky and walked away.

Eight

I was always borrowing cars from Joe Galliger's Car Lot. Sometimes I paid him for their use; sometimes I didn't. If it looked like I might get them banged up, I gave him money and collected it back if I returned them undamaged. This wasn't Joe's idea, but mine. Joe would let me use any car I wanted, disregarding his moaning and groaning about me abusing his 'cream puffs'. This time, I was just going to see the Little Sisters of Charity and check out an address that was probably vacant. I didn't figure much would happen to the car, so I didn't leave him any money.

I didn't select the fastest car on the lot. The car I selected could move if it had to, but I thought that a V-8 Ford or

Mercury could outrun its 85-horsepower, 6-cylinder block engine. Ford and Mercury were currently producing V-8's with over a hundred horsepower. Even the 6-cylinder new 1953 Chevrolets had over a hundred horsepower in their block engines. I figured a Merc. or Ford would take the Chevies anytime, but I wasn't going for speed on this trip. I wanted beauty, and that's why I chose a 1950 Studebaker Regal Delux 2-door sedan that was an off-maroon with white side walls.

What made the Studie such a beautiful car was its bullet-nosed front and wrap-around rear window. In the front it didn't really have what I considered a grill. Sticking out in the middle where a grill usually went was a round chrome piece on what looked like a bullet casing. In the middle of it was another chrome piece that stuck out like a bullet in a shell. It was like the bullets I had fired in my M-1 rifle in Korea, but this was a beautiful silver-color instead of bronze and brought pleasure instead of death. The chrome headlights, sticking out from each fender, made me feel like the car was being shot out of a cannon. A solid chrome bumper completed the bullet-nosed front, and with the wrap-around rear window that afforded great visibility in looking out the back of the car, I thought the Studebaker had a look of the future that was right out of Buck Rogers.

Studebaker had jumped out with a revolutionary car design after World War II with its '47 models. By the early fifties, Studebaker was selling well.

This was a spectacular comeback for a company that had almost gone belly up during the Depression. One of its chief executives had committed suicide in the thirties when the company was in financial crisis.

Personally, I hoped Studebaker would be around for a long time to come, since they produced some of my favorite cars. For a company that had started out making covered wagons in the 1850's, they were doing well as automobile makers in the 1950's. I expected they would still be going strong in the 2050's, long after I was gone.

I felt good as I left the car lot at a little after seven in the morning. "It's just like old times." was my reply to Joe's, "Be careful, Marty. That's a real cream puff." He would say something was a cream puff even if it was a bucket of bolts that was long overdue for the scrap heap. In the case of the '50 Studebaker I was driving, the term 'cream puff' was accurate. With a careful one-owner who had only put a little over 18,000 miles on it, the car was like new, and it handled like new. I turned on the radio, picked up Nat King Cole singing, and settled in for the ride of a little under 1100 miles to the City of Angels.

The mountains were aflame with yellows, reds and oranges. The aspen were golden and ran up and down canyons like rivers of gold, reminding me of the yellow mineral that had built this state, along with silver.

The Rockies are the backbone of the country and as I climbed higher and higher into the mountains, the Studie taking the switchback curves with ease, I knew I was in God's country. What did New York, L.A., or anywhere else have that could match the majesty of these mountains? The mountains climbed up in evergreen pine and spruce until they reached timberline where nature said, "That's high enough. Beyond this point, we don't need anymore trees, just craggy peaks, covered with boulders." It was as if God had been shucking peanuts and cast the husks down onto the tops of the great mountains where they lay in erratic piles and contorted shapes.

As I went over Loveland Pass, bogged down behind a trucker who had to take his semi around the curves real slow, I wondered if anybody would ever cut a tunnel through the mountain. They had talked about it and maybe someday it would happen. If it did happen, motorists would miss the beauty and grandeur of the top of the pass, but it would speed up traffic and take some of the danger out of crossing the Rockies in winter.

When I hit the open stretches in Utah I gave the Studie its freedom to run. I was in Mormon country. They had claimed it, settled, and carved a state out of the wilderness. They knew about freedom and the need for big government to keep its nose out of people's business. The Studie and I were one and the same with freedom. We were running hard and fast, a blend of man and machine, bouncing in short glides off the pavement. I almost expected to fly into the air, climbing into the lazy, fluffy white clouds that drifted aimlessly across the beautiful powder-blue sky.

Then I heard the motorcycle siren. I looked in the overhead mirror and saw the rider that had probably cut into the highway right after I passed and was rapidly falling back. I glanced at the speedometer that was jiggling around ninety. I thought I could outrun him, but since I was so far from the Utah-Nevada border, he would probably radio ahead, and unless I wanted to try to fight my way out of Utah, I had better stop, which I did. The motorcycle cop was red-faced, either from the high speed he had been traveling or from anger. His square jaw was quaking a little in what I interpreted as definite anger as he unzipped his black motorcycle jacket.

"Going a little fast, aren't you?"

"I guess I just got carried away with the car."

"Yeh, it's a beaut, all right. Let's see your license."

I pulled my wallet out of my hip pocket and retrieved the driver's license. It had expired while I was in Korea. I decided I had bought myself big trouble and would have to face the consequences.

"How come you haven't renewed this?"

"I was in Korea when it expired."

"How long you been home?"

"Less than a week."

"What branch of the service were you in?"

There was hope. Maybe my luck was running good.

"Marine Corps. I had a buddy of mine that was from Utah, Sergeant Kritchfield. Didn't drink, didn't smoke, didn't swear, but Kritch was a damn good Marine. One of the few Mormons I ever served with. Never could quite figure him out. There was all this death, destruction, profanity, whoring around, and he was never much affected by it."

"What happened to him?"

"He got hit when we were in the Punchbowl. I think he survived, but I'm not totally sure."

He handed the license back to me. "Semper fi, pal. Hold it down, or here is one Mormon former-Marine who is going to bust your ass."

"Semper fi, pal, and thanks."

The nice thing about being a Marine is once a Marine, always a Marine--and a lot of cops had been in the Marine Corps. Maybe there is an affinity of busting up the bad guys in the world to busting up the bad guys at home. Whatever the reason, I was grateful and I did hold the Studie down to about sixty the rest of the way to L.A.

I spent the night in Vegas, turning in at about 2 a.m. The town was growing. The downtown area had major gambling attractions, but an area called 'The Strip' had really taken off since the last time I was there. The Flamingo, the Desert Inn, the Thuderbird, and the Sands were up and running, and other hotels and gambling palaces were under construction. I figured Vegas for mob money at work.

Gambling is a sucker's bet, so I stayed away from it. After a steak dinner, I knocked back some bourbon and water while watching a lounge show.

I got to L.A. the next afternoon and checked into a motel. I decided that it was too late in the day to start business, so I shaved, showered, ate dinner and went to a Humphrey Bogart movie. I liked to check Bogie out once in awhile so that I would know how us tough-guy detectives are supposed to act.

The next morning after breakfast at a coffee ship I drove the Studie over to the Little Sisters of Charity. I had checked with Harry Makris before leaving home, so I knew the Mother Superior had approved of my visit and was expecting me. Although she greeted me sternly, I felt that she was friendly. She wore a black habit with a white hood and looked about sixty. We looked at photo albums and school picture books in her office.

There wasn't any luck with current members of the order and current teachers and students at the school. I scanned pictures for about fifteen minutes without success.

A 1944 picture of girls graduating from high school changed my luck. One of the girls was 'Sister Brochetti', only she wasn't 'Sister Brochetti'; she was 'Lucile Brodrick'. Her 18-year-old face was youthfully beautiful, but there was no doubt it was the same face as the beautiful 27-year-old 'nun' I had met on the train and later saw kneeling at the grave of Frank Brodrick.

I pushed the photo book across the desk to the Mother Superior. She had been patiently sitting in her high-backed, wood chair while I thumbed through each set of pictures she had kept pushing across the table to me as fast as I could go through them.

"Lucile Brodrick," I said, "class of 1944."

The Mother Superior looked at the photograph. "Strange. Just yesterday I had an inquiry about her from two men. This is the girl you say masqueraded as a sister from our order?"

"She called herself 'Sister Brochetti'. Did the two men who inquired about her ask for Lucile Brodrick of Sister Brochetti?"

"Lucile Brodrick. There was no mention of a Sister Brochetti."

"What were the two men like?"

"Fairly rough looking, but polite. I could give them no current information on her. That's all they seemed to be interested in was where they could locate her. When I couldn't help them, they left."

"When was the last time you saw her, if ever you saw her?"

"Of course I saw her. I have been a member of the order for thirty-two years. She was one of my students before I became the Mother Superior. A bright girl, with better-than-ordinary academic skills, she thought about becoming a member of our order. I advised against it; at least at the age of 18. She seemed far too unsettled at that time to become a nun. I told her to experience a little of life, and then if she felt the same way in a couple of years, to come back and I would help her with her intention of devoting herself to God."

"Did she ever come back?"

"She never did. So many of our girls keep in touch with us after they leave the school. She never did."

"How long was she here?"

"From the age of 5 until the age of 18."

I quickly did a calculation in my head. "That would mean she came to you in 1931. I expect she was not an orphan."

"She was not. She had a father who said he could not rear her after her mother died. He visited regularly, three times a year."

"I know, April, July and December."

"That's right."

"And his name was Frank Brodrick."

"Right again." She smiled. "You are a good private detective, aren't you?"

"I like to think so. When was the last time you saw Frank Brodrick?"

"The year she was graduated from high school. That year he came out at the end of May for her graduation. He was most grateful and made a large contribution to the order; that in spite of the fact that he had given generously for his daughter's support and care during the years that she was here."

"Where did Frank's wife die?"

"Where? You mean in what city?"

"Yes."

"I think he and his daughter came from New York City. Then he moved to Denver after he left her with us. We had a telephone number for him, but, as I recall, we were instructed to call it only in case of an emergency. He must have been a very busy man. Is he still in Denver?"

"He's dead, Mother Superior. I think that may have something to do with why Lucile Brodrick was masquerading as a nun and why those two men were here looking for her. Frank Brodrick was murdered and I think somebody thinks Lucile knows something they don't want told. She is probably in hiding, and those two men that you saw are probably part of the group that is out to get her."

The Mother Superior looked genuinely shocked. "My goodness, who do they think they are, trying to harm one of our girls?" I liked the way she assumed a protective attitude to a woman who hadn't been one of her girls for nine years. The Mother Superior and the Little Sisters of Charity were O.K.

"Well, I don't think you will hear anything more of them since you don't know where Lucile Brodrick is. If they do return or anyone else comes looking for her, or if Lucile Brodrick should come to see you, call Detective Harry Makris in Denver. If anybody gives you any trouble, call your local police."

"What about you, Mr. Mayfield? Will you stop back by and check on us?"

"I've found out what I wanted to know. I'll be heading back to Denver tomorrow after I check out one other thing. You have been most helpful, Mother Superior, and I sincerely appreciate it."

"You will do what you can to help Lucile, won't you, Mr. Mayfield?"

"I'll do my best. I don't go to church much, but I'm not adverse to any help I can get from prayer. Say a little prayer for Lucile Brodrick and I'll do my best."

She smiled again and this time the smile was radiant. "I'll do my best, Mr. Mayfield, and you do your best."

Nine

Frank Brodrick's West Franklin Street address was empty when I arrived, but cigarette butts in ashtrays in the living room, kitchen and bedroom indicated that someone had recently been there. Some of the butts were fairly fresh and the house smelled strongly of smoke. The cigarettes were all the same brand and most of them showed traces of lipstick. The house was a Spanish-style sand stucco that had been built before World War II. On a tree-lined street, the little house and moderate-sized yard looked picturesque. The lock on the back door had been easy to pick.

I settled in for a wait and smoked a few cigarettes myself. I sat in the moss-green easy chair that matched the moss-green drape on the picture window. My view from behind the edge of the drape enabled me to see the front yard and the street in front of the house. I had parked the Studie on the other side of the street and down a little, which let me look at its beautiful bullet nose during my long wait.

After about five hours I was tempted to go get a hamburger, but I stayed with it. I was rewarded a mere hour and twenty minutes later when Lucile Brodrick came walking up the walk, a brown paper bag of groceries in her arm. It was almost dark.

I crouched by the side of the easy chair as she fumbled with her key on the outside of the door. I didn't want to frighten her as she came in. I preferred to not have to chase her down the street with her screaming.

She opened the door, walked through the living room and into the kitchen without noticing me. She sat the bag of groceries on the counter by the sink and switched on the light. I walked up behind her.

"Hi, Lucile; remember me?"

She jumped and turned around.

"Relax. It's only me, your train buddy."

"Cripes on a crutch, Sergeant Mayfield. Do you have to scare me like that and what are you doing here?"

"You mean 'Christ on a crutch', don't you? I'm private detective Mayfield now, and I tried not to scare you."

"I meant 'Cripes on a crutch'. It keeps me from swearing if I use phrases like that."

"I suppose 'shoot' goes for, well, I won't say it, but I think I get the idea. While we are playing semantics, how did 'Lucile Brodrick' turn into 'Sister Brochetti'?"

She opened a kitchen drawer and pulled out a partially-smoked pack of Kent cigarettes. I lit the cigarette for her with my Marine Corps lighter.

"You smoke too much," I said.

"Tell me something I don't know."

"I'll tell you some things I know that you don't know I know. You are Frank Brodrick's daughter. He brought you out here from New York in 1931 and left you in the care of the Little Sisters of Charity. He visited you regularly for Christmas, Easter, and when you were out of school in the summer. You left the Little Sisters of Charity at the age of 18 in 1944. What you have been doing since then I don't know, except I do know you stayed in California, because Frank continued his visits up until the time of his death. Unfortunately, someone killed your father and you loved your father enough to go to the funeral, even though you knew there was danger to you personally. The mob tried to snatch you at the funeral. I stopped them from doing so and you showed your gratitude by running back to California without giving me a chance to help you. Now it's your turn to tell me what I don't know."

She took a deep drag on the Kent and exhaled slowly, giving herself time to think. "What were you to my father?"

"I rented a room at the Pig and Poke and then your father and I became friends. I was living at the Pig and Poke at the time I decided to go back into the Marine Corps. I came home and heard about your father's death. Your father always treated me square and I would like to nail his murderer and help his daughter in any way I can."

"You don't want to get mixed up in this. These people are dangerous."

"O.K., Lucile, tell me something I don't know. First of all, what have you been doing since you left the Little Sisters of Charity?"

"Trying to be an actress."

"Having any luck?"

"Bit parts here and there. A couple of good roles at a local playhouse. A couple of walk-ons in the movies. I've never made much money, but I keep plugging away. My father sent me money to live on. The house is paid for and in his name, so I haven't been too expensive. I wait tables at a greasy spoon, which helps with the expenses, which is where I was until I came home tonight."

"What do you know that the mob doesn't want you to tell?"

"I honestly don't know why they want me. I know that before we came to California, my father was some kind of gangster in New York City. As a little girl I didn't know this, but when I graduated from high school, he said there were some things he should tell me. He didn't tell me much, just that he had been a gangster in New York and wanted to turn over a new leaf when my mother died. The only way he could get out of the gang he was in was to run away and change his name."

"So, his name was really 'Brochettie', as is yours?"

"That's right. His real name was Frank Brochetti. He became Frank Brodrick and I became Lucile Brodrick. Lucile is my real name."

"As a 5-year-old you must have known your name was 'Brochetti'. How did he get you to accept the name 'Brodrick'?"

"He told me it was a game we were playing. He said there were some bad people after us and it was very important that we never let them know our name was 'Brochetti'. The nuns called me Lucile Brodrick, so it was easy for me to accept the new name in a new place with all new people."

"Did you ever hear him mention the name of any of his former gang-land associates?"

I asked him once about what he had done. He said, 'Honey, you don't want to know. After I left boxing I worked for a man called Joe the Boss. We did bad things and I wanted to get out of it. I think those were his exact words. As an aspiring actress I have to be good at learning my lines. I usually pick up on what people say. I remember that exactly because it made a profound impression on me. My father was always so gentle and kind with me. I could never think of him doing anything bad or illegal."

"Well, that doesn't sound like much of a reason for the mob to want to grab you. Maybe they think your father told you more than he did or maybe there is something we are overlooking. Whatever the case, they found out that you are Frank's daughter and they are actively looking for you. That means we have to find a way to keep you safe until we can figure out what it is they think you've got or we nail them. How did you know you would be in danger when you came to Denver?"

"My father told me never to come to Denver to see him, and he said that if he ever died, to be very careful if I came to his funeral. I thought playing the role of a nun made sense."

She had butted out her cigarette and was reaching for another. I put my hand on her wrist and stopped her from pulling another cigarette out of the pack. "Actresses shouldn't be so nervous. It might make you forget some lines."

"Mayfield, get your hand off me. I'll smoke when I want."

"I'll bet you will. I don't normally put any restrictions on anybody's behavior but my own. Maybe since I found out that you are Frank's daughter, I feel kind of big-brother protective of you."

"After what we did on the train, you feel like a brother. Mayfield, you're sick."

"Well, you know what I mean."

She smiled teasingly. "Do you need another treatment to make you feel less like a big brother?"

"Is that an invitation?"

"Could be. The first time I justified it by telling myself you were a lonely Marine who had done a patriotic duty for his country and deserved a proper welcome home. Actually, I didn't want to admit that I was lonely myself, scared, and despondent over my father's death. This time, I don't know that I could justify it."

I raised her arm from the kitchen counter and pulled her into my arms. "I came all the way to California to help you." That wasn't the total truth of my visit, but I thought it was worth a try.

"Good point," she replied noncommittally.

"It might help calm your nerves," I suggested.

"I'm weakening."

"You don't want me to go on feeling like a brother, do you?"

"Could I respect myself in the morning?"

"If you felt we cared about each other, rather than just an act of passion."

"I don't know you that well."

"You are getting to know me better all the time."

"Oh, shut up and kiss me," she demanded.

I complied willingly. After I kissed her I picked her up and carried her to a bedroom.

"Not this one, silly. The other one."

I took her into the other bedroom and put her down on the bed. After kissing her a couple more times we undressed. It was as good as the first time, even without the rocking motion of the train.

When we completed our lovemaking we smoked in bed and tried to decide what was the safest thing for her to do.

"Have you got anyplace you can stay besides here?" I asked.

"What is wrong with here?"

"The Mother Superior told me that a couple of guys were at the school trying to get information on your current whereabouts. They were probably mob from the way she described them. If they got to the school, they might get here. So, how about it, can you stay anyplace else?"

"Would I be safer back in Denver? I'll have to go back

there to settle my father's estate."

"Not yet. Give me more time to figure out what is going on. The mob will be looking for you to show up to claim your father's property. I'll let a friend of mine on the police force know that you are the heir to the estate. He can get probate court or whoever is handling the disposition of the estate to hold off for awhile. If we can nail the mob for your father's death before you get back to Denver, it might be a lot safer for you. Anyplace other than here that you can stay?"

"I have a friend who lives over near Topanga Canyon. She is trying to be an actress too. She has wanted me to move in with her to share expenses, but I've always preferred staying here. I'll call her."

I watched as she got up off the bed. Growing up in an all-girls school hadn't made her shy about displaying her body. She remained naked as she dialed the telephone that was on the table by the bed.

"Rhonda, Lucile. How are you?"

I listened as they chitchatted about acting and work. Lucile continued to stand, giving me a side view of her well-proportioned body as she shifted her weight from leg to leg. After about ten minutes, the arrangement was made. Lucile would move in on a temporary basis. They would both try the arrangement to see how it worked. Lucile wouldn't be bringing all of her things over at first, just a suitcase to let her get by for awhile. Lucile would be over in the morning.

Hanging up the telephone, she turned to me and said, "How was that?"

"Excellent."

"You're not bad yourself," she said, scooting back onto the bed and kissing me.

Before I could get my motor running again, she pushed me away and said, "I'm going to shower. Want to dine in or out?"

"If you had a full day of working in a restaurant, you

probably don't want to cook; then again, maybe you would just as soon stay away from a restaurant."

"I'll take that as an invitation, not a very definite one, but I'll take what I can get. There is a new place I would like to try. It is called 'Denny's'.

"With a name like that, I doubt that it will last long, but you're on. Probably just some little guy trying to make it like all the rest of us. But I'm all for little guys having a shot at their dream."

"A private detective with a heart--I'm impressed."

"Don't be; I just figure with a name like 'Denny's', it will need all the help it can get. Why didn't the owner call it 'Flaming Francois' or something that might have a chance of making it?"

"Probably because his name is 'Denny', that's why."

"Oh," I said.

Denny's wasn't where the tuxedo set ate, but I liked it.

Ten

I didn't notice the 1953 black 4-door Cadillac following us until we started winding into some little hills outside of L.A. There wasn't any other traffic on the dirt road at 9:15 in the morning, so the Cadillac was easy to notice. The driver was real good. I figured the Cadillac would have had to have picked us up at Lucile's house.

Maybe it was just that I was sloppy careless. Being around a beautiful woman can sometimes do that to a guy. I should have observed my rear-view mirror more than Lucile's bare ankle and foot. She had deposited her black flats on the floor and was sitting with her bare right foot under her left leg that went down to the floor to her empty shoes. Even though it was the first part of October, L.A. was summer-hot. Lucile had on a pair of jeans and a loose-fitting purple sweater. My motor hadn't totally calmed down from the night before, so I was acutely aware of her presence. Too bad I hadn't been that aware of the Cadillac that had decided to tail us.

"Lucile, don't be obvious, but I want you to glance over your shoulder and tell me if you have ever seen that car or the two guys you can see in the front seat."

After a casual glance over her shoulder, Lucile said in a voice that was calmer than I expected, "Never saw them or the car."

I speeded up the Studie, testing if the Caddie would keep the pace. It did.

"Are you familiar with this area?" I asked Lucile as I leaned the Studie around dirt curves that churned up dust.

"Not very, only that it goes up and then down towards the ocean."

"Don't worry. Their car is faster, but ours corners better." Forty was as fast as I could let the Studie run at any one time up the road, but we were staying ahead of the Caddie.

My view of the Caddie in the rear-view mirror cleared enough through the dust for me to see a handgun being thrust out the front of the car opposite the driver.

"Get down!" I pushed Lucile's head down with my right hand. The warning came just in time as the wrap-around window in the back crumbled and a bullet hole appeared above the dash on Lucile's side of the windshield.

"What the fudge are they doing!" Lucile yelled from her bent-over position.

I didn't answer as I weaved the Studie back and forth across the road and cut the curves as fast as I could. Shots were still being fired from the Caddie, but my weaving and the dust were keeping them from having any degree of accuracy. If a bullet hit something, it would be chance.

I could see the ocean as we started to descend. I didn't

have any time to absorb its beauty as I cut the Studie in and out, skidding around curves, and pushing it when I could.

"O.K., you bastards," I hissed through my clenched teeth as I saw my opportunity. The Studie had maneuverability. The Caddie had speed. I was going to use the Studie's maneuverability to nullify the Caddie's speed. We were going to kick ass.

I spun the Studie around on the wide part of the road that had been created as a place to park and look down at the ocean a couple of hundred feet below. I gunned the Studie back up the road. The Studie squeezed by the Caddie on the hillside of the road. They had no more interest in a head-on collision than I did. I caught a glimpse of three faces as they flew by, two in the front seat and one in the back. It was too fast to register their mood or state of mind.

As the driver of the Caddie was jamming on the Caddie's brakes, creating a dirt cloud, and swinging into the overlook to turn the Caddie around, I cut the Studie onto a side road that went to somebody's hillside house. I jammed on the Studie's brakes, creating my own dust cloud, and backed up. I knew I could turn the Studie faster than he could turn the Caddie.

"What the hay is going on!" Lucile shouted as she continued to bounce wildly between the floor and the seat, still trying to keep her head down.

"We're going for the kill baby!" I pointed the bullet nose of the Studie toward the Caddie. "Roll yourself into a ball on the floor and protect your head! Hang on!"

The Caddie was completing its turn. It had gone forward and back a couple of times and had almost pointed its massive lumbering black hulk back up the hill. The guy in the back seat was firing his rod at us from the left side of the Caddie as I closed the distance.

I ran the bullet nose of the Studie into the left front fender of the Caddie as I jammed on the brakes and cut the Studie a hard left. There was a thunderous sound of bumping and scratching metal.

Both cars performed magnificently, as cars should. The front of the Caddie spun to the right. The Studie bounced to the left and stayed on the road. As the Studie stopped in a cloud of dust, I heard the Caddie go over the side and crash down the hill. I was glad I couldn't see it. I hated to waste good cars. I heard the explosion and saw a flash of flame shooting up from beside the road where the Caddie had taken the big fall.

"Holy crutch, Mayfield! What the fudge have you done!" I cut the engine of the Studie. The silence and lack of movement felt good. My hands were shaking as I started to get out of the car. "Come on, Little Sister of Charity. Let's see if there is anything left of our bad guys."

Lucile got out of the Studie with a mixture of caution and stretching pain. She wobbled on each leg as she slipped on the shoes she had reached back inside the car to get. "You ace hole," she said as she examined her body for missing parts. "You fudging near killed me."

"It couldn't be helped. They damn near killed you." I started to walk back up the road. Lucile followed dutifully.

The Caddie carcass was burning on the beach below. It hadn't quite made it to the water's edge. The turquoise water, more blue than green, was rolling in gentle waves onto the sand as if whatever had just happened didn't matter. The sea gulls, skimming the water and puttering around on the beach, were walking and squawking as contentedly as ever.

"Got a cigarette, Mayfield?" Lucile asked as we stared down at the smoldering Caddie and expanse of beautiful ocean.

"It's not your brand."

"I know, but mine are back in the car."

I reached up into my left shirt pocket and for the first time became aware of the pain in my left side. It was probably in the crackup that I had cracked a rib or two.

I lit her Lucky with my Marine Corps lighter and then lit mine. I noticed blood on her face.

"Your lip is bleeding, kid. Anything else damaged?"

"I don't think so. How about you?"

"I'm in good shape. Let's get the hell out of here before we have to explain it to the cops."

"Thank you, Holy Mother and Holy Father," she said and crossed herself.

"If you said 'fudge' one more time, I thought you might have to say a few Hail Marys."

"Go fudge yourself, Mayfield."

I chuckled and we walked back to the Studie. I gave it only a quick inspection, but I thought it was O.K. There wasn't anything dripping from under the car--a busted right headlight, a bent-down chrome front bumper, a shot-out wrap-around rear window--the thing I hated most about the damage was the blunted bullet nose. I knew the Studie would still roll if the right front tire could roll without scraping the bent fender.

"You did O.K., little Studie," I said as I fired up the engine. "You took care of the big, bad Caddie."

"Do you always talk to cars?"

"Only when I feel like it."

"You know, Mayfield, you may be a little weird."

I listened for scraping as we started down the hill. I heard none, so I knew the Studie could still perform. "Good girl," I said.

"Why am I a good girl?" Lucile asked.

"Not you, the car."

"You may even be sick, rather than just weird."

"Who knows? I love beautiful women and beautiful cars. Is that a crime?"

"Only if you don't know the difference."

"I know the difference, but I love to hear both of them

purr. A car is like a beautiful woman. Usually, if you treat a fine car or a beautiful woman with respect, they'll never let you down. Once in awhile it doesn't work that way because you get a lemon, but that's just the way it is with cars and women. On the other hand, if you treat a fine car or a beautiful woman badly, they'll give you nothing but misery. A guy who slaps his woman or damages his car when he doesn't have to is a fool."

"And you certainly know how to take care of cars," Lucile said as she ground her Lucky out in the car ashtray. "Look at this one and the one you just knocked off the road."

"You do what you have to do."

I saw her reach for one of her cigarettes that had come out of the Kent cigarette pack that had bounced off the seat during the chase and may have miraculously survived being crushed on the floor. "You smoke too much, kid."

"Just putting it back in the pack, wild man."

I laughed even though it made my left side hurt.

"Mayfield, as a private detective, do you do this type of thing often?"

"What's that?"

"Fighting with bad guys, protecting people, and smashing up cars."

"It goes with the territory. Sometimes it's just a twisted world, and I try to make a living straightening it out. As I said, you do what you have to do."

Eleven

With Lucile deposited, hopefully safely, at her friend's house near Topanga Canyon, I pointed the blunt nose of the Studebaker towards Denver. I didn't want to hang around L.A. long enough for the cops to get nosey about my dented car. It was going to be hard enough to explain to Joe Galliger what had happened to his cream puff without having to explain it to California cops who would probably hold me for an inquest into the deaths of the guys I had bumped over the cliff. I decided that a quick departure was my best defense against involvement.

I was driving straight through, but in Utah I had an involuntary stop. The same motorcycle cop I had encountered on the way to California was still on the job. This time it wasn't speed that concerned him, but rather the condition of the car. He pulled me over just about daybreak when the giant red rock formations were beginning to come out of the shadows into a yellow-orange sun. I turned off the engine and tried to look cheerful.

"Hi, pal," I said. "It's me again. I've been holding it right at the speed limit all the way."

"It's not your speed that bothers me. What happened to the car?"

"Let's just say I had an accident."

"That's an understatement."

I nodded my head in agreement.

"I remember you," he said, as if a sudden revelation had just come to him.

"You should; I just came through here a few days ago."

"Not that." He snapped his fingers as he pointed his left finger at me. "A few years ago, I think it was 1949."

I hoped whatever he was remembering was good.

"You were the guy who crashed through the border at Tijuana while chasing that guy who had been involved in killing a woman in Colorado. There were those Communist agents on the train. Martin Mayfield, that's it, private detective. You got national publicity out of it."

"I guess I was famous for a day or two."

He touched a finger to the bullet hole in the windshield and I knew an explanation would be required.

"Give it to me straight; what happened on this trip?"

"I went to L.A. to check out a lead on a murder case that happened in Denver. After following up my lead at a Catholic orphanage, girls' school, I protected the daughter of the murder victim by running some mobsters off a cliff. That's totally straight."

"What did the California cops say?"

"I left before I had a chance to find out. No publicity, no

investigation, just three dead mobsters found at the bottom of a cliff in a demolished Cadillac. I shouldn't have told you this, but since you gave me a break on the way out and we both know what semper fi means, I figure I can trust you. I'm heading back to Denver to try to nail the murderer. You ever hear of anything called the MAFIA?"

"Yeh, just lately. Those Congressional crime investigations turned up the heat on organized crime. I don't suppose we have any of it here in Utah, but I hear it's a criminal group that operates on a nationwide basis. They got anything to do with the murder your investigating?"

"I think so, and I think they just lost three of their boys to the nose of this Studebaker that pushed a black Cadillac over a cliff."

He walked around the car, looking at the damage and thinking. I didn't interrupt his thoughts.

"Well, Mayfield, I'm turning you loose again, even though it would be usual police procedure to hold you for questioning. See if the next time you come through my state you can do it without breaking any laws."

"You got it," I said and started the engine.

He stuck out his hand toward the open car window for a handshake. "Good luck," he said as I extended my right hand across my chest and stuck it out the window, even though the twisting of my body hurt my cracked rib or ribs.

"Don't they teach you guys not to do this sort of thing. If I pulled a gun, this could be dangerous." I shook his hand.

"They teach us. I just figure that whether we like it not, we kind of ended up buddies, Mayfield."

"You got it, MacDonald," I said, reading the name on his black motorcycle jacket.

"Dave MacDonald," he said.

"I'm Marty. I'll catch you the next time I come through Utah. I'll buy you a drink--no, I guess I won't," I said, remembering his Mormon religion. "Maybe a cup of coffee?"

He chuckled. "Saints aren't big on coffee either, but we'll work it out the next time you come through."

"We'll work it out," I said and pulled the Studebaker back onto the highway. He gave me a motorcycle escort with siren for about five miles and then it was on to Colorado where I hoped I wouldn't have to do much explaining of the car.

When Joe Galliger saw the car in late afternoon as I pulled onto the lot, he groaned. He didn't say anything, but I knew he wanted to.

"Sorry Joe," I volunteered. "I'll pay for the damage if I've got enough to cover it. It couldn't be helped, but it sure saved my bacon."

"Jeez, Marty," Joe said irritably, his efforts at controlling his anger starting to unravel. "What happened and did it have to be this bad?"

"You remember our 'nun'. It saved her life and mine. That a good enough tradeoff for the damaged car?"

"It sounds necessary."

"You see me here today only because of this car."

"I'll put it in the body shop. I imagine it won't cost you more than five hundred, providing there is no damage to the motor." He saw the bullet hole in the windshield. "It will cost more than five hundred. Rough trip, huh?"

"That's what I been trying to tell you, Joe, rough trip."

"You wouldn't consider taking a train or an airplane the next time you have to go someplace?"

"I might," I said, thinking that I might have to go to New York to try to get whoever had ordered the killing of Frank Brodrick. I figured the hit for local talent, but the order probably came from higher up, if there was a nationwide crime organization, which people kept telling me there was. Since Frank had come out of the New York mob in the days of old, that was probably where the order to hit Frank had originated. I wondered what Delana had found in her research of organized crime. I had asked here to dig, and I knew she would, coming up with whatever she could.

I looked forward to seeing Delana. I hoped I didn't feel guilty after my involvement with Lucile. Things just seemed to happen between women and me, and I never quite knew how or why. From past experience I have learned that it was best not to analyze my romantic entanglements. It was better just to let it happen as it happened.

One of the things I liked about Delana was that she was independent enough to let me be independent; yet, we had what I considered a deep relationship, as long as I didn't slip up and tell her what had happened between Lucile and me in L.A. I may have not been the brightest güy when it came to understanding a relationship with a woman, but I wasn't fool enough to think you told them about other women.

Twelve

It was flicking snowflakes outside when I dropped into the Rocky Mountain News to pick up Delana for lunch. The snow wasn't much, a dry October thing with the temperature hovering around thirty and spitting big flakes off an on. When you had to worry was when October hit you with a wet one that was a combination of rain and snow. That usually turned the streets to glass. This one had just enough cold in it to make me switch to my heavy gray sports coat, which I combined with blue slacks. It still wasn't cold enough to force me into a tie, which usually happened in late December or early January. I hoped the cleaners had gotten the mothball smell out of the sports coat.

"Hey, Mayfield, win any more wars?" The voice was Jimmy Delong's and he was still wearing a stupid red bow tie. He was a few feet away, sitting behind his black typewriter. This time we hadn't attracted an audience yet.

I walked over to his desk and reached my right hand to his bow tie. "Just as I thought, a clip on," I said quietly, unsnapping it. I used my left hand to squeeze his mouth open while I stuffed the bow tie in with my right hand. "Chew on that for awhile, Jimmy, and you may learn to keep your mouth shut. You open that uncontrolled big mouth of yours again and I'll stick a fist in it. You understand me?"

He nodded, since the bow tie in his mouth and my hand holding his jaw prevented him from speaking.

"Marty, over here," Delana called. "I'm ready."

I released my hand from Jimmy's jaw and let him pull out the bow tie with his fingers. He placed it beside the typewriter on the desk. I smiled over my shoulder at Delana. "I'm on my way. Jimmy and I were just having a friendly chat." I frowned at Jimmy. "Weren't we?"

Jimmy put his balled hand to his mouth and coughed, probably as a result of over-salivating and nervousness. Removing his hand from his mouth he said, "Yes."

"Yes, what?" I asked.

"Yes, we were having a friendly chat." He didn't sound like he really meant it, but that was good enough. I smiled and Jimmy forced a smile when I looked at him.

Delana, in one or her dark-blue, heavier suits, walked toward us. "Glad to see you boys are getting along."

Delana and I went to the Tea Room. It was close to her paper and was a pleasant mixture of class and comfortable ordinary. Downtown shoppers and office workers could drop into the Tea Room, which was over a department store, and enjoy reasonably-priced, elegant dining in a comfortable way. The place was interesting to me because of its ability to be up-scale and ordinary at the same time. With green, potted ferns and white tablecloths, it had a feeling of elegance, and the people who dined there were usually nicely dressed. Yet, at the same time, an office worker on a tight budget could feel totally at home having the soup of the day and a sandwich. Even as huge as the Tea Room was, seating maybe five or six hundred, it had a feeling of intimacy.

"How was Los Angeles?" Delana asked as our coffee was poured from a silver tea kettle into delicate white cups with a blue flower pattern on the side. Doing the pouring was a waitress in a green uniform. I waited until the waitress left before I answered.

"I found out some interesting things. Our 'nun' is really not a 'nun', but the daughter of Frank Brodrick. Nice kid, just trying to be an actress." I purposely made Lucile sound younger than she was, as if she were maybe fresh out of high school. "The mob was looking for her, so I stashed her at one of her friend's house, not really a house, more of a cabin with a loft over it. They are a couple of kids, trying to be actresses. Frank took her to California after her mother died and put her in a Catholic girls' school. He skipped out to California three times a year to see her. The mob thinks she knows something important, but she doesn't know what it is. She knows her father was in the mob in New York years ago, but that is about it."

"Can I print any of it?"

I gave her an annoyed look. "What do you think?"

"No, I guess not. But that is my job, so it doesn't hurt to ask."

"You will get it all when we've got it all. We are getting closer, sweetheart, so I think we will get it all. What have you got for me?"

I contacted some people who were involved in the Congressional investigation of organized crime. I got some transcripts of the hearings, but I don't think you want to wade through them. I've pulled out what I think you need to know.

Perhaps the most important thing I found out is that Frank was probably one of the unnamed witnesses who testified at a closed-door hearing. Many of the hearings were open to the public, giving committee members a chance to puff their egos. Makes great stuff for the press and voters--Senator so and so fights crime. But some of the hearings were closed-door with witnesses not identified to the public or in the transcripts. From the testimony given, I think Frank was one of those witnesses."

"That is terrific, Delana; now we have a motive. Good work!" I was so enthusiastic I almost spilled the coffee I was drinking from the delicate cup that was one of those that never have a big enough handle for guys with big hands--but what can you expect from a 'tea room'?

"I thought that information would please you, darling. Frank testified, giving information incriminating mob members. Thus, the mob wanted to kill him, which they probably did."

We were interrupted by the waitress bringing our food. I had a hot roast beef sandwich, since I've always been a meat and potatoes sort of guy. Delana's order was more adventurous--roast duck and Waldorf salad.

"What did the testimony show that Frank knew?"

"I think it was Frank, but I can't be totally sure. There was other corroborating testimony, but what I picked up as being specifically Frank's was that he had followed his fight career with jointing a New York gang. That's how I identified the person as Frank, the boxing background and a later move to Denver when he quit the gang."

I nodded my head in approval.

Delana continued, only occasionally taking a bite of food: "In the early thirties the gangs that had come out of Prohibition had a war in New York. Luck Luciano eventually emerged as the top man, but he was initially just a member of Joe the Boss Masseria's gang. The guy that I think was Frank was also a member of the gang of Joe the Boss. In the testimony they sometimes didn't call them 'gangs'; sometimes they called them 'families'. When Joe the Boss was killed, Frank fled New York. He would not reveal specifically what he had done while he was a gang member. All he would say was that after all of the killings and gang warfare, he wanted to get out of it."

"Was there much in the testimony about a nationwide organizational structure called the MAFIA?"

"When reading the transcripts of the hearings, you piece it together. One witness gives a bit of the picture, somebody else, something that you add to the total picture."

"So, what is the complete picture, as far as you know?"

"The MAFIA is an imported criminal organization from Southern Italy, specifically Sicily. In Italy they were known as 'Men of Honor' in their local villages and provided a buffer between the ordinary citizen and harsh government or ineffectual government. As time went on, the organization became more criminal in its activities. Exporting it to this country was a natural thing when you had millions of Italian immigrants pouring into the United States around the turn of the century. The immigrants were unfamiliar with the American practices of law and government that had grown out of English tradition. The immigrants were greeted with big-city machine politics and bosses. Add on the money and opportunity that existed during Prohibition through selling illegal booze and you've got the Italians reaching out for their slice of the pie, following the same method of operation they had in Italy--strong family ties with the 'Men of Honor' looking out for Italian interests."

"You would make quite a schoolteacher, Delana," I interrupted.

She frowned as if she had heard a distasteful idea, which she had. "I would never be a schoolteacher. That is O.K. for some people, but not for me. I'm a reporter, and I love the sense of freedom it offers me. Can you imagine me cooped up in room all day with kids?"

"No, I guess I can't. So anyway, what is the MAFIA like today?"

"It is organized across the country in major cities. It is rumored that there is a national meeting every five years. They still have a blood-brother type of thing, with Sicilians being in the inner circle. They take an oath of silence, which may be what got Frank killed. They don't let you ever disavow that oath of silence; once a member, always a member, which, as you can see, may have caused problems for Frank. First, he ducks out on them, and then years later turns up testifying before a Congressional committee and breaking the code of silence. Very naughty, indeed, from their point of view."

"Then it would be possible for a New York crime family to order a hit through a local crime family?"

Delana thought a minute before answering. "I don't know, but I think so. Frank's testimony was about the crime families in New York, so I imagine the New York families could have ordered Frank's death."

"You said 'families' rather than 'family'. You mean there is more than one MAFIA crime family in New York?"

"The testimony indicated that there are five. It is very strange. They divide the city into various parts or operations, with each family having control over a particular type of crime or area. Sometimes they fight over who controls what. That is what happened when Frank was in the MAFIA. They kill each other off at times; yet, they know each other intimately and have long periods of peace when they work together. They can be talking and kissing each other on the cheek one day and brutally killing each other the next day. It is a strange mixture of deference and violence. New York has five crime families because it is so big and the city has a long history of corrupt politics. Across the country there may be as many as twenty-some crime families. Denver probably only has one crime family, if it has any."

I thought of Fat Georgie and Sam Vitaliano. "I think it is safe to assume Denver has a crime family. I figure the MAFIA does numbers, any and all kinds of gambling, prostitution, narcotics. Anything else?"

"Oh yes." Delana looked pleased with herself. "I thought you might want to know some of the activities they undertake. They sometimes put money into or control legitimate enterprises. Sometimes the line between 'illegal' and 'legitimate' becomes very thin. Boxing might be one example."

"Damn, I've always liked boxing. You mean organized crime controls it?"

"According to committee testimony, managers and promoters of some of the top fighters and fights in the country have some very unsavory backgrounds. When you have mob figures controlling fighters or fights--well, you draw your own conclusions."

"What else is the mob into?"

"Would you care to try labor unions? Some unions are honest and operate in the interest of the members. Others are completely controlled by the mob. It's a good bet that the New York docks were under the control of the mob even during World War II. First, the Irish gangs had control of the Longshoremen's union; then the Italian MAFIA moved in. By the 1940's, Lucky Luciano, who had been shipped off to prison in the thirties, was probably able to make a deal with the federal government for his release from prison that would take place when the war ended. Prohibition gangs had been run off by the Italian MAFIA. The MAFIA got in bed with politicians--you may have heard that politicians can be bought. In spite of a reform mayor like Fiorello La Guardia and a racket-buster like Thomas Dewey, the mob had control of the New York docks during World War II. With men like you fighting the war, the shipments out of New York were vital if we wanted to win the war."

"Those bastards. You mean supplies to guys who were fighting and dying in Europe for the cause of freedom were being squeezed by the mob?"

Delana tried to soothe my anger. She put a hand across the table and laid it on my wrist.

"Luciano probably did get a surprise. If the story is right, Liciano provided labor peace and security to the New York docks after a mysterious ship fire that lost one of our biggest ships. In return for his wartime cooperation, Luciano was released from jail, but to his surprise, he was promptly deported, which merely meant that he would run his crime family from Italy rather than from New York City. If he could run it from prison, he could run it from Italy. He has wanted to get back into the country ever since his deportation, but the government had said, "no dice'."

"Any other unions, besides the Longshoremen's union, that are controlled by the mob?"

"Now, don't jump to conclusions about the Longshoremen's union, darling. The West Coast branch of it may be controlled by the Communist."

"Great. You have the East Coast docks controlled by the mob. You have the West Coast docks controlled by the Communists. It almost makes me feel that my fighting for democracy was worthwhile."

"I said, 'may be'. In the union movement you've got some people crying 'mob' and other people crying 'Communist'. Quite frankly, I don't know what to believe. In my opinion, it is a good bet that the mob is in the Hotel and Restaurant Employees' union, the Teamster's union, the Laborer's union, and the Longshoremen's union of the East Coast."

I managed to not swear, but that really made me mad. I had sweated with my hands enough in life to know that a guy shoveling dirt didn't need his own union stealing from him. On the one hand, the poor sap had his employer squeezing him for as much work as he could deliver as cheaply as the employer could get by; on the other hand, the mob was squeezing him for the just rewards of his labor. The thought of all this made me madder than hell, but I controlled my tongue, sitting in angry silence.

"Finished with your food, darling?" Delana asked, trying to sound cheerful. "Maybe I'm too good at researching."

"I'm finished," I said, knowing it sounded sour, but trying not to take my anger out on Delana. "You are a wonderful researcher. I'm not mad at you; I'm just mad at the people who are screwing the system up."

I wanted to say more, but I didn't, figuring it would sound too--whatever. I wanted to say that I believed in the Constitution, the Bill of Rights, the flag, and the U.S. Marine Corps, and I didn't like it when cheap hoods or anybody soiled them. I wanted to say that I didn't like it that Frank, who had made some mistakes, but had changed and lived a decent life, had been cut down by this thing called the MAFIA. I needed to avenge his death and fight this octopus of crime. I knew you could never kill it, but maybe it could have some of its tentacles chopped off. I felt all this and maybe I wanted to tell Delana some of it, but all I could do was stare into my empty coffee cup with the too-small handle.

"Hey, darling," Delana said, bringing me out of my thoughts. "Don't you think we ought to get out of here? I've got to get back to the paper."

I smiled at her. "Sure." I knew that was enough. She would know I appreciated her and her research.

Thirteen

After I walked Delana back to the Rocky Mountain News I went to see Harry Makris. I wanted more information about the octopus. What I heard was that the octopus had claimed another victim--Paulie Lovatto. His head had been blown off with a shotgun in exactly the same manner as Frank had been murdered. The location was even the same--the tunnel in the Denver Coliseum. It was obvious that the mob was trying to send a message to any and all to leave hands off the Frank Brodrick murder case. Paulie Lovatto, Frank's checkers-playing buddy, would never spill to me or anyone else.

"Damn, Harry, he was about to talk. I was giving him a little time to simmer and then I was going to try him again.

Did you get anything from him?"

"How was I to get anything from him? It would have been nice, Marty, if you would have clued me in that you thought he was about to reveal something."

"I'm sorry, Harry. I guess I should have, but it's a little late now."

"Very late," Harry said, clearly annoyed.

"He had a checkers-playing buddy named Carlo Lambini. He was the third one in a threesome with Frank Brodrick. They all belonged to this checkers club that meets at Berkeley Park. Frank is dead; now Paulie Lovatto. Maybe we had better get to Carlo Lambini before somebody else does. Then again, maybe he is the leak that fed the mob information, first, about Frank, and then later that Lovatto was getting ready to spill to me. What do you think?"

"Let's go upstairs. I'll see if I can find an address on, what did you say his name was, Carlo Lambini?"

"Yeh, Lambini. Since you are Italian you shouldn't have much trouble spelling it."

"Maybe I'm Greek today. I haven't made up my mind. What are you driving today?"

"Gray '50 Ford 2-door, only a six-banger, but a nice car, still pretty hot."

"Five to one he lives in North-Denver Italy. If he is mob related, maybe we will do better driving your car. They can spot a police car, marked or unmarked, from fifty miles away. Your car will be less-conspicuous and we might have better luck in getting him to talk to us. Any objections?"

"None, other than what Joe Galliger might have if we get his 'cream puff' banged up."

"Official police business; it's covered for any scratches we might put on it."

I hoped Joe would understand if I tore up another car, but I doubted it.

One the way to the North-Denver address of Carlo

Lambini I filled Harry in on what had happened in California, with two notable exceptions: I didn't tell him that Lucile Brochetti and I had enjoyed bedroom pleasure and I didn't tell him that I had deposited the three hoods at the bottom of a cliff in a flaming Cadillac. I didn't want to explain it to the California cops and I didn't want to explain it to him. I also sketched for him what Delana had just told me her research had revealed about Frank and the mob.

"It's all beginning to make sense," Harry said with the same look of satisfaction I had exhibited when Delana had told me the results of her research. "That lady is so terrifically smart. She is probably too smart for a guy like you, but I still think you should marry her."

"It goes through my mind occasionally, Harry, but every time I add it up, it comes out the same way."

"How?"

"That we are better off this way, attached, but not attached."

Harry gave me a look of 'You are too dumb for her', which I ignored.

Carlo Lambini lived in North Denver--solid, old-line, middle-class, Italian. The two-story, red-brick houses were as solid as Denver itself, going back to the 1920's and earlier, before track homes, which had been taking over the Denver market since World War II, were fashionable. We walked up the cement steps onto the large cement porch with large overhanging roof and pressed the door buzzer. I was surprised that Carlo Lambini was at home, and that he opened the door himself.

"You should be more careful, Carlo, before you open doors," I said. "We could have been some of your mob friends."

The remark did not bring a denial of mob connection, as I expected. Instead, he said, "I knew it was you. I had you made from the time you stepped out of that gray Ford. But what does it matter?"

"What do you mean it doesn't matter?" Harry asked. "I'm Detective Harry Makris of the Denver Police Department. May we come in and talk?"

"I know who you are," Lambini said sullenly, his thin mouth on his thin face curling down in disdain under his thin pepper-gray mustache. He wore black stacks, a black shirt, a red sports coat, and a light blue scarf hanging in front of the shirt, but wrapped up high around his neck. I thought he dressed pretty well, except he reminded me of what I thought a Hollywood movie director would look like. His pepper-gray hair was combed straight back, as it had been when I had seen him at the checkers club.

He glanced up and down the street. "Come on in before we all get blown away--first, Frank and now Paulie."

We went inside and he bolted the door. He motioned us to sit down on the maroon sofa that sat on a glistening hardwood floor. A round rug of intricate design, with purples, reds and blues, was on the floor in front of us and in front of the maroon easy chair in which he sat across from us. A varnished black desk was next to the arch leading into the dining room where I could see a long table with high-backed wooden chairs. He saw me noticing the furnishings.

"Pretty good, huh?" My wife before she died--God rest her soul-- she ran a pretty good house. Now I have a maid come in twice a week."

Harry said, "You seem to know why we are here, Mr. Lambini. What can you tell us about the deaths of Frank Brodrick and Paulie Lovatto?"

"Frank Brochetti," Carlo said with an almost mystical look. "Frank Brochetti was his name, not Frank Brodrick. He never should have changed it."

"Why did he change it?" Harry asked.

"He changed it to protect his daughter. He didn't want his past to ever touch her."

Harry's voice was calm and reassuring as he asked. "What else can you tell us?"

"Ready for a surprise, Mr. Detective? I'm going to spill it all. I'm a stoolie--I spilled to the mob where Frank was--I spilled to the mob that Paulie was going to talk to Mayfield--I'm the stoolie, and now I'm going to spill to you."

He stopped talking and looked at us, and then he stood up and began pacing agitatedly in front of us. "You are surprised, and you want to know why I'm spilling to you now. Because I can't stand to look at myself in the mirror, that's why! They were my friends and I got them killed. I swore an oath a long time ago, an oath of loyalty and silence. I never broke that oath. Frank broke that oath, and Paulie was about to break it. I stayed true to La Cosa Nostra. You two know what La Cosa Nostra is?"

He stopped pacing and looked at us. His head was cocked to the side and he was baring his lower teeth in an almost demented manner.

We nodded and then he went back to pacing--agitated, tormented, a man who was obviously facing his own guilt. When he said nothing, Harry stood and placed a hand on Lambini's shoulder. "Why don't you just sit down, Mr. Lambini, and try to tell us about it?"

Carlo looked at an old photograph that was hanging on the wall. It showed a young couple, dressed in what looked like wedding clothes. "Lucia, now I make it up to Frank and Paulie, and you." He sat down in the easy chair and Harry continued to stand.

"Mind if I smoke, Mr. Lambini?" I asked, thinking that I might calm him down a little by getting him to think of ordinary things.

"Help yourself," he said as if I weren't even there. I lit a Lucky with my Marine Corps lighter and listened to Carlo Lambini's story as I smoked and flicked my ashes into the standing ashtray at the end of the couch. Cigarette smoke was never one of Harry's favorite things, and I noticed him over by Lambini moving even further away to avoid the smoke.

"We grew up together," Lambini said, his mind reaching back over the years. "Frank, Paulie, and me, we were inseparable. Frank was always the big, strong one. Paulie was always the good-natured, funny one. I was the wiry, tough little one who didn't take no crap from nobody. They gave me crap, and I busted them. If I couldn't bust them, Frank busted them for me. We were dirt-faced kids who swam in the East River, stole from the street vendors, slept on the fire escapes to get out of the heat and stench of our crowded family quarters. Our mothers cared; our families cared; but somehow the three of us went astray. Men of honor, ha! We thought we were men of honor, when all we became was street punks. Frank almost made it out; he was a boxer; he even came out here and boxed a little; that's how we knew about Denver."

"How did you get involved with the MAFIA?" Harry asked, trying to give Lambini's life story some focus.

"Prohibition. Money, the clubs, wild times and good times, but then killing times. Frank the Enforcer, Paulie the Jokester, and Carlo the Shark--do I look like a shark? Those were our names. The family has names for its members. It gives you identification and respect."

"Did you break from the mob at the same time as Frank did?" I asked.

"Sure, the three of us did. Joe the Boss had been killed. There was fighting among blood brothers. We didn't like or trust Lucky Luciano. He was letting in that Jew Meyer Lansky. Sicilian, that is who you can trust."

I said, "Yeh, sure, look what happened to your two friends and who did them in."

The remark was like a shot between the eyes to Lambini. He went red with anger and then white.

"Don't you think I know what I've done!" he shouted, trying to get up, but Harry pushed him back in his seat. He was breathing hard and he held his left arm straight, with his right hand coming across and holding his left arm above the elbow. Mixing with his look of anger was a look of pain.

"Calm down, Mr. Lambini." Harry said quietly. "Are you O.K., Mr. Lambini?"

Lambini nodded, but continued to hold his left arm with his right hand.

Harry went on in a calm, quiet voice. "We know you are sorry about what happened to your friends. It was an ethical decision, being true to the code you had sworn to uphold or being true to your friends."

"Damn the code," Lambini said, his voice just above a whisper.

I figured we had better work fast if we wanted anything coherent out of him. I thought he was on the verge of an emotional collapse, a physical collapse, or both.

I said, "So, you, Frank, and Paulie split from the New York mob and laid low out here in Denver. How did the Congressional committee get Frank to talk?"

"They found out he had a daughter he had been hiding in California. The Feds threatened to tell the mob about her if he didn't testify."

"He testified and then you--" I wanted to say 'ratted on him to the mob', but I didn't. "Then you lived up to the oath you had sworn as a young man and told the mob that Frank had testified."

Lambini nodded. He appeared more relaxed and he stopped holding his arm.

Harry asked, "How did the mob get Frank to the Denver Coliseum?"

"Told him that if he wanted his daughter to live, that he had better show up there."

I asked, "How did they know he had a daughter?"

Lambini started to cry. I didn't wait for an answer. "O.K., so after you told them Frank had a daughter, they shot Frank and then when Paulie was going to spill to me, you again lived up to your code and told the mob about Paulie. Paulie was killed as a warning to anyone who had an interest in finding out who killed Frank to forget it. Is that right?"

Lambini nodded, gaining control of his tears and trying to look like the tough mobster he had been in his younger days. He took a white handkerchief out of his sports coat pocket and pretended to blow his nose when he was actually wiping his eyes.

I ignored his movements with the handkerchief and went on. "What I want to know is who did the shooting?"

"Fat Georgie and the two soldiers who travel with him. I don't know who actually pulled the trigger. There may have been another soldier in on it."

Harry looked puzzled. "You mean military men?"

"No. For a smart cop, you can be pretty dumb. In the family, guys who do the jobs are called 'soldiers'."

"Who ordered the hit?" I asked.

"You met him."

"You mean me--I met him?"

"Yes, you Mayfield. The guy who gave you the Cadillac when you were in New York trying to get the guy who killed that girl a couple years back, before you went back to the Marines."

"You mean Irene Hampton?"

"How should I know? All I remember is that Frank made the connection with Jake the Snake Macella for you. You went back there and came back with a Cadillac. Frank was pretty proud that you pulled that off. Even Paulie and me had a little respect for you out of that one. We thought for sure you were going to get yourself bumped off. We gave Frank two-to-one odds on a fifty-dollar bet. When you came back alive, it cost Paulie a hundred and me a hundred. Jake the

Snake must have liked you to give you the Cadillac."

"He said he liked war heroes. He thought there was something special about me being in the battle for Iwo Jima in World War II. He said if I ever came back to New York he would blow my head off. Real friendly guy."

"Are you going now that you know who ordered the hit on Frank?" Lambini asked.

"I'm going."

Lambini gave me a look of satisfaction.

"No, you won't," Harry said forcefully. "We've got Mr. Lambini's testimony and we'll nail them with the law. With Mr. Lambini testifying, we can nail Fat Georgie and this guy Macella. You will testify, won't you, Mr. Lambini?"

"Oh, sure," Lambini said nonchalantly. "The law can take care of Jake the Snake, Fat Georgie and me." He smiled. "You know how good the law is at getting us criminals. I'm as guilty as Jake the Snake and Fat Georgie. You will be able to protect me until the trial, and I will testify. It is as simple as that." He smiled again, and I knew he was mocking Harry, figuring that the law could never protect him from the vengeance of the mob long enough for him to testify.

"Let's go downtown, Mr. Lambini. We'll get a sworn statement from you and we'll put you in a safe place with police protection."

"Sure, Detective Makris. Just let me get my medicine to take with me; bad heart, you know. I've got some tablets in that desk over there. Nitroglycerin tablets help me when my heart does whatever it is the doctors say it does."

As I saw the .45 come out of the black desk drawer I sprang off the couch and made a running dive for Lambini. His arm movement was as fast as my leg movements. He blew his brains out with one shot to the side of the head just as I tackled his waist. I ended up on the floor with my arms around a dead man, with bone, brain, and blood splattered all over me. Harry almost threw up as he watched me untangle myself and get up.

"There goes your witness, Harry," I said, trying to mentally distance myself from what had just happened. I had found that if you blotted a horrible event out of your mind as soon as possible, you could get through it and deal with it later. With brain and bone fragments all over my clothes and face, mixed with fresh blood, it took my maximum power of concentration to deal with the situation.

When Harry could not reply, I continued calmly, "I'm going to New York after this Jake the Snake. Keep it under your hat until I get back. In the meantime, see what you can do about nailing Fat Georgie. We know he did it, so all you have to do is find some way to legally pin it on him. If you can't find anything to get him with while I'm gone, we will work on it when I get back. O.K.?"

Harry nodded.

"I'm still staying with Joe Galliger. I'll go over there and clean up. When you and your brother officers have tidied up over here, maybe you and I can have a drink at the Red Horse. I haven't had time to drop in there since I got back."

Harry nodded again and reached for the telephone on the desk, presumably to call headquarters. "You'll have to stick around for awhile, Marty. I'll need your statement when other officers get here. I don't want to leave any doubts that this was suicide. We came to question him; he told us nothing; he went over to the desk, pulled a gun, and blew his brains out. That is all I want said about it."

"O.K., Harry. My nerves are shot to hell, and I want to get out of these clothes, but do what you need to do. I agree with keeping what we found out quiet. That may help in nailing Fat Georgie."

"And, Marty, I really don't know who I can trust other than you, even on the force. Sam Vitaliano has so many guys on his payroll, I even have doubts about my captain. I haven't got anything specific connecting Captain Garret to the mob, but some things just don't add up. He is either less-than-competent or he is protecting the mob. I know we could be arresting people involved in numbers, but Garret isn't pushing it. Just you and me, buddy--we keep it quiet."

I lit a Lucky as I watched him dial the police station. I sat down on the couch and smoked, trying to become unaware of the brain, bone, and blood that covered me and my clothes. I thought about Frank, Carlo, and Paulie swimming in the East River when they were kids. Now all three of them were gone. As we run our race with life, we never know how it is going to turn out. I was sorry it hadn't turned out better for the three of them.

Fourteen

The Red Horse was one of those places that never change. You could go there anytime, any day and it was always the same. Depending on when you went in, there were less or more people, but the place had an ageless quality, as if it were suspended between yesterday and tomorrow. It was always friendly, always dispensing cheer, comfort, advice, or whatever you needed.

Bountiful Beverly waited inside, behind the outer red walls that had the red stallion flying over the entrance. She and Red were always there, Red in his sixties, pot-bellied, no trace of the red hair he once had before his head had gone bald, wearing a white T-shirt, a white cook's hat, no matter what the weather outside. Beverly, in her forties, always wore a sweater and slacks. Her ample breasts gave the male patrons viewing pleasure, as did her dyed blonde hair. The curl of double chin and her short flat nose did not matter, nor did her sensuous mouth and brown eyes. What mattered was the warmth she dispensed--comfort, sex goddess, she was all woman, and she generated femininity, even when displaying a tough exterior.

"Marty!" she yelled as she came from behind the bar and squeezed me in a smothering embrace. The guys staring at us from the bar did not matter--it was only the two of us, standing between the red-cushioned booths and the red bar stools in the open floor that was where the ordinary met.

I let her kiss me long and hard, before prying her arms from me. "What's wrong, Beverly, you run out of guys to sell bourbon and water to?"

"I heard you were back, Marty. Bourbon and water coming up--and whatever else you want." She let the 'whatever else you want' linger, making sure I got the full meaning of it.

"Harry and I need a drink. Coors for him and a Shirley Temple for me."

She stepped back and looked at me. "Shirley Temple?"

"Just kidding. Red around?"

"Sure; I'll get him."

"Tell him not to show up until he brings me steak and eggs. I want black coffee with the meal. I'll need four eggs, over hard, and a big steak. He knows how to cook it. You hungry, Harry?"

It had taken the rest of the afternoon to finish the police reports and get cleaned up. At ten minutes until seven I was hungry. I figured Harry would be the same.

Harry shook his head and said, "How you can eat after what we have just been through, I don't know."

"Still old Mr. married sourpuss," Beverly said, playfully

sticking her tongue out at Harry.

Harry laughed. "Still married, and still what--a sourpuss? You haven't improved your disposition any either."

Beverly stuck out her tongue again. They bantered like this, but is was all in fun. She stuck out her tongue to me and wiggled it a little.

"Just remember, Marty, anything you want," she said, obviously not referring to the food and drink.

"Maybe later, sweet cakes. Harry and I need a drink and I'm hungry as a bear. I'll let you know before I leave."

As Harry and I sat down in the booth and waited for our drinks he said, "Marty, how can you encourage her when you have a doll like Delana?"

"Ever bury yourself in a pair of 44's?" I asked.

"You've got a point."

He said no more about Beverly, but I could see him glancing at her, trying not to be obvious.

"Kind of makes you wonder, doesn't it, pal, even a married guy?"

"I love my wife," Harry said defensively.

"Of course, you do. I think I am in love with Delana, but it doesn't mean we've died."

"I see what you mean."

As we had our drinks I turned the conversation to less-pleasant things, chief among them being Jake the Snake Macella. "Got any ideas on how I can get him legally, Harry?"

"No, but I'll think about it."

"Think about it all you want, and it will still come up zero. He's sitting back in New York City, insulated from the law out here and he has bought protection by cops back there."

"Maybe the Feds," Harry suggested.

I started to laugh and he joined me.

"I guess you're right, Marty. Maybe I can make a

connection someplace and pull a little weight."

"Yeh, you go on thinking that and you and Macella will be long dead before anything happens."

"What are you trying to tell me, Marty?"

"If there is no way to take him legally, I might have to figure out something else."

"Nothing illegal, Marty. I'm a cop and I'm sworn to uphold the law."

"I didn't say 'illegal'; you did. I'm not telling you anything, but if something happens to me, I just want you to know I tried to do it legal--but sometimes legal just doesn't cut it. It's a twisted world and a guy does what he has to do."

"Why go at all?"

"Frank was my friend; that's why. Furthermore, I learned from Delana that while you were getting your ass shot off in Italy during W.W. Two, our mob friends were putting a squeeze on the New York docks to get Lucky Luciano sprung from jail. I figure I owe the New York mob a visit from both of us."

"Is that how Luciano got sprung?" Harry was clearly surprised.

"That's what Delana's research shows is probably the case."

"O.K., Marty, I don't want to hear anything; I don't want to know anything. I'm on the right side of the law, and I want you to stay on that side of the law too. If you break the law, and I know how it happened, I'll have to bust you."

"Fair enough, Harry. We never had this conversation, and you don't know anything."

"You're right--I don't know, and I don't want to know. I think you are a damn fool for going, but I know I can't stop you, short of putting you in jail temporarily on a trumped-up charge. I wish you luck, old buddy, and I hope you will be careful."

"As careful as I was on Iwo and at Seoul. As careful as

you were in North Africa and Italy. We kicked ass, Harry, guys like you and me. We are not going to let somebody else have the damn country."

"I know, pal; that's why I'm an honest cop."

"Hell, Harry, I'm leaving tomorrow morning for New York. Let's drop the shop talk. How about another beer?"

"O.K., but I need a hamburger to wash it down, or is it the other way around? You know what I mean."

"Beverly!" I called, "bring my sourpuss friend another beer and tell Red to cook him a hamburger, well-done."

Beverly nodded from where she was taking another order at the bar.

"How did you know I wanted it well-done?"

"I remember, Harry."

"I could have changed while you were away."

"But you didn't, right?"

"Right."

About fifteen minutes later, Red ambled out from the kitchen area, carrying a tray. He unloaded the food in front of us and then stuck out his hand. "Welcome home, Marty," he said as I shook his hand. His gray eyebrows hadn't changed. The red freckles on his face, neck and arms seemed the same. It even looked like the same white apron, white T-shirt and white cook's hat, even though I knew they weren't.

"How do you and Beverly do it, Red?"

"What?"

"You are the only two people I know who never seem to grow any older."

Red smiled, revealing yellow teeth with one missing on the lower front. He chewed tobacco, so the stained teeth were understandable. Since he was smiling, I figured he wasn't chewing at the moment.

"You look a little older, Marty."

"Thanks, Red. I wouldn't want to come back from fighting a war and not look older. How come six eggs instead of four?"

"Homecoming, Marty. When I came back from World War I, people did nice things for me. I thought it would be nice to do something for you."

We were interrupted by Beverly bringing hot coffee. Harry said to skip the coffee for him, preferring to continue nursing his beer. Beverly purposely leaned her breasts close to me as she poured the coffee. When she left, Red went on with his account of World War I. I scooted over in the booth and let him sit beside me. He started out by telling us he had been a little older than some of the guys in World War I.

"I was 31 when I went. I wanted to get off the farm for awhile anyway, and I guess I wanted to, as they said then, 'make the world safe for democracy'. Those were Woodrow Wilson's words."

"What do you think, Red, did you?" Harry asked.

"Maybe for a day or two. But look at what has happened since then. You and Marty had to fight another war, and then Marty went off to do it again. Seems like there's always somebody wanting to take it away from us. And this last one I don't even understand. They should have let MacArthur bomb China. That's right, isn't it, Marty?"

"That's the way I figure it, Red." I said while cutting a big chunk of the porterhouse steak. "But they never ask guys like you, Harry and me. We just do it as best we can, no matter what the damn politicians say or do."

Red looked very serious as he said, "I'm glad you're O.K., Marty. I got gassed in my war--exploding gas shell damn near killed me. My whole body seemed to swell up and I damn near went blind. War isn't much fun."

"Mind telling us how it happened?" Harry said.

"Damn mule, that's what it was. If that damn mule would have moved, I wouldn't have been gassed."

Harry was falling into his role of a questioning cop as he asked, "What mule? What did the mule do?"

"Wouldn't move, that's what," Red said, still seeming

mad at the mule after thirty-five years or so. "We needed mules to pack supplies and sometimes help in other ways. Well, we were trying to pull this truck out of the mud--terrible mud over there on the Western Front. Damn mule decided to sit down--you ever hear the expression 'stubborn as a mule?"

We nodded.

"Bastard wouldn't go on. I figure we could have been out of there ten minutes earlier--then I wouldn't have got gassed. While I was fooling with that damn mule, the Heinies lobbed a gas shell and it exploded right beside the truck. The whole thing was the mule's fault and I never wanted to see a mule again. That's why I never went back to the farm after the war."

"But, Red," I said, "maybe that mule was just as sick of the war as you were. Maybe that's why he sat down."

"Never looked at it that way," Red said, mulling the situation over. "Maybe I shouldn't have been so mad at the mule, but just the same, I think it was his fault. That's why I named this place the 'Red Horse', just to show that damn mule that I thought more of horses than I did of mules."

Harry chuckled and I smiled.

"It weren't so damn funny," Red said, probably more angry at the mule than he was at Harry and me thinking it was amusing.

Harry immediately looked serious. "Sorry, Red. I didn't mean it was funny, you getting gassed. I just thought it was kind of funny how it happened--a mule and all."

"Yeh, I guess you're right," Red said, sounding less-than-convinced. "Well, I got to get back to the kitchen."

"How come you haven't got a cook on at this time of the evening?" I asked.

"They either quit or I fire them. I'll probably hire another one in about a week or two; then he'll screw up and if he don't quit, I'll fire him. Most of them aren't any better than that damn mule. Beverly is the only good help I ever had."

We agreed and watched him shuffle back toward the kitchen. The steak was a little tough, but good. Harry ate all of his hamburger, which told me that it must have been pretty good, since Harry was fairly particular about what he ate.

As we were leaving I leaned over the bar and quietly said to Beverly, "I'll have to pass. I'm heading out in the morning, so I need a good night's sleep. I can't wait around until you get off work."

Barmaids were usually the most inconvenient women in the world to fool around with. They usually didn't get off until around two in the morning and then they sometimes wanted you to buy them breakfast. By the time you waited for them and got through the preliminaries, you were usually so tired that it wasn't worth it. They usually weren't too fresh themselves, and in the bright lights of an all-night cafe, they seldom looked as good as you thought they did in a dimly-lit bar.

Beverly bent down behind the bar and I could see her fumbling in her purse. She unobtrusively slipped me a key. "Same place, Marty, if you're interested. Sleep until I get there."

With an offer like that and the thought of Bountiful Beverly, I didn't see how I could refuse. As I took the key and slipped it into my sports coat pocket, I winked at her. Harry didn't say anything as we left the bar, but I could tell that his mind was alternating between thoughts of envy and condemning me for not being exclusively committed to Delana.

"What the hell, Harry," I said as I dropped him from the gray Ford at his track home that looked just about like all of the other track homes of his neighbors, "it was a long war."

"Sure, old buddy. But when you get tired of fooling around, maybe you will wise up and marry Delana."

I watched him go into the house and wondered if he

wasn't right. It might be nice to be going into one of those little houses, with Delana waiting inside for me. Then I thought of Bountiful Beverly. It was never easy to resolve life's complex issues.

Fifteen

I parked the Ford outside the trailer house and let myself in with the key. I didn't think it necessary to hide the car or my presence.

I had been there twice before, so the surroundings were not unfamiliar when I turned on the light. I didn't notice anything that had changed in the last three years. Everything was clean, neat, and in order, from the hanging potted plant to the knickknacks and pictures on the shelf.

There were no pictures of Beverly's former husband, but there were several pictures of her daughter who was in college the last time I had been there. I calculated in my mind that since she had just finished her freshman year in

1950 when I had gone back to the Marines that she might have finished college by now. There it was, her college graduation picture, next to her high school graduation picture. There was also a picture of Beverly and her daughter taken at the graduation ceremony. Beverly was dressed up and had her arm around her daughter who was in a black graduation gown, with the traditional hat that hardly ever sat properly on the graduate's head. The daughter was a thinner version of Beverly, but taller than her mother. They both looked happy, and it made me glad.

It made me glad because I liked to see little people getting joy out of life. Beverly was not the rich and famous. She was one of the little people across America, living their ordinary lives, doing ordinary things. A job, a college graduation, the hope of the future--this was what it was all about: Red in his white cook's hat, hating that mule forever; Harry doing his police work and going home to his little track house and his wife and three kids; Joe running his car lot and me borrowing cars and sometimes tearing the hell out of them; Delana working at the paper and always trying for the big story. Damn, it made me feel good, just thinking about all of it.

We worked and we struggled, sometimes making mistakes, but it was all worth it when we did the best that we could at whatever we wanted to do, whether we made anything out of our lives or not. As long as we lived it in a way that made sense to us and tried not to hurt other people unnecessarily or without just cause, we could be proud of our lives. It was sometimes a twisted world and we did what we had to do, but it was also a beautiful world when ordinary people could live their lives in peace.

Beverly would come to me in the night. Two ordinary people, we would enjoy a caring moment. We would love and be loved in a physical way. With the physical love would be a higher love of sharing and caring. It would not be a cold night in Korea, hunkered down in a slit trench, wondering when the next wave of attackers would come. There would be no flashing rifles in the night, sending bullets of death. There would be no warm blood from a buddy, pumping from an artery I was desperately trying to tie off with a tourniquet to stop the flowing away of life. There would be no eyes glazing over as death neared. There would be no screams of pain and curses of anger and fear shattering the night. Tonight, there would only be the warmth of Beverly's body.

I heard her come in even though she came in as quietly as she could, doing everything from closing the door slowly with two hands and removing her shoes before walking. With a dim night-light being all she snapped on, I could still see the outline of her body as she undressed. I heard the shower running and waited in anticipation.

When she crawled into the narrow, built-in, wall bed beside me, there was no need to talk. My body was naked, as was hers, hers still having the moist warmth of the shower, mine coldly dry. Together, the moist warmth and the cold dry blended, our hearts beating faster in excitement as the urgency of our bodies took over.

Beverly crystallized my thinking on one of the truths of life that I had suspected all along: Women don't lose it as they get older--they just learn how to use it better. Buried in Beverly's magnificent breasts, I spent one of the best nights of my life.

Sixteen

I drove the gray '50 Ford Custom Tudor sedan with black walls to New York. I thought about taking an airplane or train but I decided that I would need transportation around New York and that a cab might lead to my being identified. As for using the subway, I was setting out to knock off a major New York crime figure. If I survived, I might need a faster exit than the subway could provide.

I settled on the gray '50 Ford Custom Tudor sedan as being about as inconspicuous as anything I could drive. Chevrolet in 1953 was ahead in overall production and sales, as it had been in 1950, 1951, and 1952. Over 398,000 Ford Custom Tudor sedans had been produced as a part of Ford's

1950 models. This compared to the over 316,000 Chevrolet 4-door Sport Sedans, which was Chevrolet's most-produced model in 1950. I knew things like this, not because I researched with care, but because I liked to browse through Joe Galliger's car books and pamphlet information when I didn't have much else to do. One of the reasons Joe and I got along so well was that we had a mutual love for cars.

I would have preferred an eight-banger, but since the gray Ford was the only '50 Ford he had on the lot, I figured the six-cylinder would have to do. I could have moved up to a '52 Ford that was an eight, but I calculated my safe return as less-than-favorable, so why cost Joe one of his more-expensive cars?

Whether I had a '50 or '52 Ford didn't matter much. The 1949 models had been the big styling change at Ford when the company had switched to a postwar body and that year they had beaten Chevrolet in production and sales. Ford had always been a company that was slow-to-change, preferring to stick with the tried-and-true until breaking through with major innovation, like the V-8 engines it started turning out on its 1934 models.

Ford Motor Company over the years had reflected the image of its founder, Henry Ford. I always thought of Fords as the car for ordinary people, maybe because Henry Ford had put America on wheels during the rural part of the twentieth century. First, it was the Model T. The 'Tin Lizzie' lasted until the 1920's when the Model A took over. In the 1930's, souped-up V-8's became police car favorites. Gangster John Dillinger even sent Henry Ford a personal note, praising the speed of a Ford Dillinger had used in a getaway. Under Henry Ford's direction, it was hard for Fords to get out of the color black, and styling changes were far-between.

At the end of World War II, when Henry Ford turned over operation of Ford to his grandson Henry Ford II, new thinking emerged. The gray '50 Ford Custom Tudor sedan that I was slogging through snows in Kansas with was the product of the new thinking. The windshield wiper clunked dutifully back and forth, keeping the heavy, wet snow off the windshield. The heater was kicking out a steady stream of heat and the radio was fading in and out with various stations as I went down the road. What more could an ordinary guy ask for?

I was driving the car of the ordinary guy, a little square in appearance, but so was the ordinary guy. Similar to Studebaker's bullet grill, the Ford grill was understated, without the real bullet affect that the Studebaker had. Frisky, but solid, was the way I would describe the Ford's appearance and feel.

Some guys complained that Fords rattled too much and that they could not match Chevrolet's Body by Fisher. The Ford I was driving was tight.

There was only a difference of five horsepower between the six and the eight, so I thought the 95-horsepower engine would do just fine when I took on the hoodlums in New York. On New York streets I doubted that it would make much difference whether my Ford had 95 horses or 100 under the hood.

The car felt nice, handled nice and was one of the everyday workhorses of the American fleet that powered the ordinary guy. Since I hoped to kick a little ass for the ordinary guy, myself and Harry included, I thought it was appropriate that I was driving the ordinary guy's car.

The car was not the problem; kicking ass was. How was I going to get to Jake the Snake Macella?

As the Ford and I went down the road, I turned over in my mind the previous time I had done business with Macella in New York. It had been 1949 and I was after the killer of Irene Hampton. Macella, whose name I hadn't known then, had held his office hours over a New York liquor store. Two hoods were stationed permanently in the store. When you got by them, Macella was surrounded at any given time by a half dozen or so torpedoes. He played poker while conducting his business. I had hit a lucky streak of patriotism when he had learned that I had been on Iwo Jima in World War II. Instead of killing me, he had given me a Cadillac and told me that if I ever came back to New York, he would blow my head off. His surroundings and attitude might present a problem when I went to square things for Frank.

If I went to the New York police, many of whom were being paid off by the mob, I would hit a brick wall, even if I found an honest cop. All I had as proof that Macella was the instigator of Frank Brodrick's murder was the word of a dead man. Carlo Lambini's last words wouldn't carry very far.

If I couldn't use the law to take Macella, maybe I could devise some sort of a trap where he would give himself away and the police could grab him. That sounded great and I toyed with it for miles, but I couldn't come up with anything. It sounded like something too much out of Superman or the Green Hornet.

I thought of stopping someplace and buying a rifle and ammunition. Taking them by surprise, and with my recent combat experience, I stood a good chance of knocking them off before they got me. If I got caught by the police, it would be the electric chair for me--premeditated murder; not a good option.

Besides, I didn't think I really was a cold-blooded killer. Just storming the place and knocking off guys at random was easier planned than done. When the reality of blowing away guys, even mob murderers, hit me up close, real personal, I wasn't sure my conscience would let me do it. Kill or be killed was one thing. Murder, even in the interest of justice, was something else.

If I could somehow get in without arousing suspicions, my chances of getting away would increase. If they attempted to kill me first, I could claim self-defense--if I lived. This would make me feel better because it wouldn't be premeditated murder. It would be Harry-Makris clean and I would still get Macella.

Then again, maybe I was being a damn fool about the whole thing. All I needed was to hole up someplace near Macella's normal route from home to the liquor store. As a sniper, I could be very effective. I could take him out without much of a problem. But, what if I attracted attention and was caught before I did the shooting? Macella would be free and I would go to jail. Mission unaccomplished. Even if accomplished, there would still be my conscience to deal with.

The 'sniper plan', although seeming the least risky to me and offering a great chance of success, was finally rejected. Instead, I settled on the 'flag plan', probably a not-too-smart plan, but I wasn't always the smartest guy in the world. I would give the bastards an even break, and then when the shooting started, it would be kill or be killed. I could probably live with that--if I lived.

I bought the flag in St. Louis. I figured St. Louis for about halfway to New York. I needed a shave, shower and a good bed for the night. I had been on the road from six in the morning until past eight at night. After checking into a hotel I told the bellboy to get me an American flag. I said I would pay the cost of the flag and add a five to it for him. I don't know where or how he got it, but by the time I stepped out of the shower, he was knocking on the door and giving me a new-looking flag. He said it had cost him five dollars. He smiled and thanked me when I handed him a ten.

I crumpled the flag that was about three-feet by four-feet and ran water over it. After wringing it out, I hung it over a chair to dry, making sure it wasn't stretched very tight. I wanted wrinkles on it. I could give it a tear or two in the morning when it was dry. A little road-side dirt would add to its appearance of having been in battle.

I found a steak house. After knocking back a bourbon

and water and consuming a steak dinner, I felt good. I listened to jazz in a nightclub for about an hour, the music being as sweet as only St. Louis or New Orleans could make it.

I declined the invitation of a black woman who was pimping for herself. “White boys don’t really know what’s good,” she threw over her shoulder at me as she walked away and pimped another ‘white boy’ who left with her.

I was tired all over when the Ford and I rolled into New York City after another fourteen-hour jaunt. I checked into the same hotel I had used four years earlier when I had visited Jake the Snake Macella. I had come out of the city alive. Maybe the hotel was lucky. I only hoped my luck ran good this time.

Seventeen

I spent part of a day staking out the liquor store. I would like to have spent an extended day, but running a stakeout of more than a few hours had too much of a risk of attracting attention. After lingering over my ham and eggs and looking out the restaurant window at the liquor store, which was diagonally down the street, I eventually left after my slow-drinking of three cups of black coffee and smoking two Luckies. From the restaurant I moved to a coffee shop four-doors-down where I had a bagel and another cup of coffee. I had never eaten a bagel before, so I thought I would try one. It was a little plain for my taste, but not bad.

During my stay at the restaurant I had seen Jake the Snake

Macella and four of his torpedoes enter the already-open liquor store at 10:06. While I was at the coffee shop, they did not leave the liquor store. After a pause at the coffee shop bathroom, I hit the street again, taking a slow stroll of about three blocks in each direction, keeping the liquor store, which was on the opposite side of the street, in sight as best I could.

I returned to the Ford, which was parked about three-quarters of a block down the street on the same side as the liquor store. For about a half hour I read a newspaper I had brought from my hotel. Then I moved the Ford, driving four blocks away and cutting back and parking on the opposite side of the street on the opposite end of the block. About ten minutes later Macella and the four torpedoes, with whom he had entered the liquor store, came out and got into the 1953 black Cadillac that they had parked in front of the liquor store.

I didn't follow the Cadillac. It was noon and I figured they would be breaking from their poker playing for lunch. They would be back after lunch. Poker playing was an important job that required dedication.

I drove around the city for about an hour, just doing general sightseeing. The traffic was terrible by Denver standards, but I enjoyed seeing the Big Apple from my car as a tourist might see it.

After I returned to the vicinity of the liquor store, I found a parking place near the ham and egg restaurant and went back into the restaurant for a roast beef sandwich. After awhile I thought I might have returned too late to see Macella and his boys come back to the liquor store, but since I saw no Cadillac parked in front of it, I was still betting they hadn't returned.

At 1:38, as I was finishing my second cup of coffee, I saw the Cadillac pull up. Macella and two of his torpedoes got out of the back seat. The other two torpedoes, who were in the front seat, drove away and they did not return until over an hour later when I was re-reading the newspaper in the Ford that I had just parked at a different place.

Shortly after they returned, two guys, who looked like plain-clothes cops, pulled up in a black unmarked Ford and went in, leaving their car double-parked in the street in front of the liquor store. They came out about ten minutes later.

I could have used another day of observation to see if this was a daily pattern, but I didn't want to risk being in the neighborhood again and calling attention to myself. Macella and his four torpedoes had come out of the liquor store when I left at 3:30 to drive back to my hotel.

I figured the two who had left for about an hour after lunch were errand boys. They probably did a daily pickup from numbers or something. Routine was at the heart of the gangster world. The plain-clothes cops probably dropped by to report and drop off money. Macella would be doing his book work after they left.

If this was the daily pattern, my best shot at Macella was when he returned from lunch. That was when he seemed least-guarded, probably two torpedoes downstairs in the store and two upstairs with him. I had an hour to get at him before it got crowded.

The next day, my suitcase was in the trunk of the Ford and I was ready to leave town. The Ford was gassed, oiled and ready to roll. There would be no going back to the hotel; I had already checked out.

I had brought my two .38's on the trip with me, the one I carried in my shoulder holster and the back-up I kept in my office safe. The back-up was under the front seat on the driver's side. If somebody broke into the car and rifled it, they were less likely to find the .38 under the seat than they were in the glove compartment. By not locking the .38 in the trunk I could get to it faster if I needed it.

I gave the Cadillac a five-minute exit time while I waited in the Ford parked about three-quarters of the way down the block from the liquor store on the same side of the street as the liquor store. The Cadillac had dropped off Macella and two torpedoes just as it had the day before. The only difference, other than a three-minute time variation, was the twenty-some-degree temperature variation. Yesterday, it had been around 50 degrees. Today, it was about 30. The day was as gray as the Ford, one of those overcast, cold, blustering days of New York when the sky doesn't snow, but an ice-wind, blowing off the water, shrouds the city.

I only wore a tan sports coat, tan slacks, and a white shirt, unbuttoned at the neck without a tie. I was underdressed for the weather but I didn't want a bulky overcoat hampering my movements.

I didn't plan on being out of the Ford too long anyway. If I walked out of the liquor store, I would be back in the warmth of the Ford soon enough. If they carried me out to a hearse, then it wouldn't matter.

Macella and his boys were dressed properly for the weather. I had looked with a little envy at their dark overcoats and hats when they had unloaded from the black Cadillac. Hoods were better dressers than I was. Dark suits, flashy ties, overcoats, and hats, they always looked respectably dressed. If clothes brought respectability, they would beat me every time.

I took a deep breath before I took the folded flag from the seat beside me and got out. When I stepped into the liquor store, one of the two torpedoes, who were manning the liquor store in non-clerk attire of dark suits, asked, "What can we do for you?"

"I brought Mr. Macella something."

I could see both of their eyes searching the folded flag for evidence of a weapon concealed inside it. Folded as small and tight as it was, they really couldn't tell much without unfolding it. From their manner I could tell that they weren't accustomed to having visitors in the store. The store was a front for their mob activities, and the locals knew to stay away.

"Yeh, what's that?" the clean-cut, Italian-looking guy in his early twenties asked.

"A flag. Mr. Macella is a patriotic man. The last time I saw him we talked about the flag on Iwo Jima. I brought him this flag from the Korean War. Tell him that Martin Mayfield brought him the flag we raised over the capitol of South Korea. He will know why I brought it to him."

Clean-cut took the flag, squeezing it with both hands to see if anything was concealed inside of it. He went up the wooden stairs that had a wooden handrail.

The other guy, in his early thirties and looking anything but clean-cut, watched me carefully. He had black crew-cut hair, a pasty-white pock-marked complexion, and a bullet head above his broad shoulders.

"You packing?" he asked, after he had sized me up for thirty seconds or so.

"Yeh, I'm packing. A .38, you want it?"

"Only if Mr. Macella wants to see you."

"He will want to see me; he likes war heroes."

My hands were down at my sides. I turned the palms of my hands toward him and spread my fingers apart in a gesture of openness to show him I wasn't doing anything but getting ready to get the .38 for him. Instead, I took a step forward and grabbed his wrists, which were down at his sides, before he could go for his rod. I kneed him in the groin and pulled my .38 from its shoulder holster as he dropped to his knees, holding his private parts.

I slapped my left hand over his mouth that had started to yell in pain or in warning to Macella, and my right hand pointed the .38 at his forehead. "No noise or your head gets a big hole," I said quietly.

The stifled yell was a pain yell and he did a good job of holding it in as his face grimaced while his body was trying to return to normal.

I pulled him to his feet by using my left hand to grab the back of his dark-gray suit coat. Turning him towards the stairs, I pushed him ahead of me, continuing to hold the back of his collar with my left hand while holding the .38 to the back of his head with my right hand.

Clean-cut was just coming out the door at the top of the stairs as we reached the wooden landing that was outside the door. He stopped when he saw the pistol pointed at his associate's head.

"Back inside, pal," I said quietly. "Nobody gets hurt. I just want to visit Mr. Macella."

Macella was seated at t a heavy, round wooden table, where he had been playing a three-handed game of cards with the two torpedoes who sat at the table with him, one on each side of him. The game had been halted and they were looking at the flag that had been unfolded and was now spread out over some of the money and cards on the table. They looked up at me as Macella said, "What the--"

"Relax, Mr. Macella," I cut in. "I just want to see you."

"Why the gun then?" he asked, showing no fear. The two torpedoes sitting at the table did not look as unafraid.

"The last time I was here, you said you would blow my head off if I ever came back. I'm just trying to give myself a little insurance that you don't do that. I just wanted to say hello before I left and see if you liked the flag."

"I liked the one they had on Iwo Jima better. We won that war."

"I liked the outcome of that one better myself, Mr. Macella."

Macella didn't look much different from when I had seen him four years before. He was still heavy-set with dark, wavy hair and pudgy fingers. He reminded me of the movie actor Edward G. Robinson. He was still chewing a fat, unlit cigar. I wondered how many of those he chewed a day.

The only noticeable difference this time from the last time I saw him was the dark-gray business-suit vest he wore under the black suit coat. Wearing a vest, suit coat and a red tie, as he was, I would have been burning up in the room that seemed warm to me. Vests must have been in with the mob because the other two guys were wearing them also. All three of their overcoats were neatly hung on the coat-rack pole next to the small window with the drawn white window shade.

"Put down the heater, Mayfield. Somebody brings me a flag and I'm not going to blow them away."

"If I put it down, how do I know you won't have your boys blow me away?"

"Nonsense," Macella said as he stood up. "You keep the gun. I'll even let you play poker. We're a little short-handed for about an hour. You got any money?"

"Not the kind of money you play for," I said, looking at the hundred-dollar bills on the edge of the flag. I lowered the .38 to my side and released the collar of the torpedo I had used as my ticket to the poker game. Macella motioned his head for clean-cut and bullet head to leave.

"I'll settle with you before you leave," bullet head growled at me while rolling his shoulders back.

"Sorry, pal," I offered in the form of an apology. "I just didn't want Mr. Macella to be unhappy with my visit."

Bullet head was still scowling as he left.

I slipped the .38 under my brown sports coat and slid it into the shoulder holster. I watched Macella carefully fold the flag in half twice and drape it over the back of one of the empty wooden chairs that was out a little from the table and facing the table at an angle.

Macella pulled a fat roll of bills out of his trouser pocket and pealed off ten of them. He dropped them on the table in front of the empty chair across from him. "Sit down, war hero. You've got money. Let's play."

I sat down and watched Macella call and deal a hand of

five-card draw, with jacks or better being the opener. I had two kings, so I opened, figuring that a hundred was what I should open with since all ten of the bills he had given me were hundreds.

I had guessed right; they each saw my hundred and then we took cards. From the three cards I drew I picked up another king. Figuring I had a winning hand I raised a couple hundred. The other guys folded but Macella saw my two hundred and raised two more. I thought he was bluffing so I saw the two and called. I was right--all he had was a pair of eights.

I saw Macella's eyes flash when I pulled in the pot. He didn't like to lose.

"So, war hero, why are you really here?" Macella asked as one of his torpedoes called the game and dealt, seven-card stud, with fives wild and nothing in the hole. As each of the cards was dealt face up, Macella and I had time to talk while playing and betting.

"To give you a flag," I said.

"That's nice of you, but did you make a trip to New York for that?"

"More or less."

"You still living in hicksville?"

"You mean Denver?"

"Yeh, hicksville, Denver."

"I'm still just as big of a hick as ever."

"I hear you smashed up that Cadillac I gave you."

"I felt bad about that. It was a real nice car, but it went over a cliff."

Macella grunted. "I give you a Cadillac; you smash it up and now you give me a flag. You wouldn't be trying for another Cadillac, would you?"

"No Cadillac this time."

"Then why the flag? You don't expect me to believe you came all the way to New York just to give me a flag."

"I wanted to give it to Frank Brodrick, but he had met with an untimely death when I returned to Denver from the Korean War."

"Who was this Frank Brodrick?" Macella probed, seeming to lost interest in the game.

"You knew him--Frank Brochetti--you had him killed."

Macella put his pudgy left hand over his cards that were flat on the table and play stopped.

"So, that's what you are doing here. You came to square it for Frank."

I put my left hand under the table and calmly reached for my shoulder holster with my right hand. "That's right."

"Take him!" Macella yelled.

I upended the table on Macella, knocking him and his chair over backwards, sending cards and hundred-dollar bills flying. I drilled the torpedo to my right in the temple as he was pulling his .45 from inside his black suit coat. The torpedo on the left came closer to getting off a shot, but I planted a bullet in his heart just as he was rising from his chair with his pistol almost drawn.

Macella did get off a shot as I leaned over the upturned table and fired. His bullet tore through my left arm above the elbow. My bullet caught Jake the Snake between the eyes, splattering bone and blood.

'Stop the bleeding; protect the wound; and prevent shock.' The Marine Corps' dictum flashed into my mind.

I put my .38 on the flag chair and began to hurriedly wrap my bleeding left arm with the flag. The arm was flashing hot pain as it bled, but I knew the bullet had not struck an artery or bone as it had passed through. Bullet head, coming through the door, interrupted my medical treatment, but the flag had gotten four good tight wraps.

I dropped behind the table and the first shot from his pistol went into the heavy wood. I picked up the .45 of the first torpedo I had plugged and fired. The slug from the .45

caught bullet head in the chest. Bullet head's second bullet was fired straight up as he fell.

"Drop it!" I yelled to clean-cut as he came through the door with a sawed-off double-barreled shotgun.

I didn't want to kill anyone as young as he was, with a whole life stretching before him, but I had no choice. As he swung the sawed-off shotgun toward me I fired, going for a head shot since his body only gave me a side target. My shot was good. Both barrels of the sawed-off shotgun sprayed buckshot into the floor as he fell forward.

I pumped another .45 slug into bullet head, figuring he was the only one who had a chance of surviving my first shot. I had probably taken him out with the first slug, but in the Marine Corps I had learned to always make sure my enemy was dead.

I looked at the .45 in my hand and decided to put it back in the hand of its owner. I cupped my hand over his hand as I knelt on the floor. The .45 jumped as the dead owner and I pulled the trigger. The shot went in the direction of bullet head.

With my right hand free of a weapon, I quickly re-wrapped the bloody flag on my left arm. It had come loose during the shooting and was hanging down, doing little good. This time I got it completely wrapped and tucked the end into the top of the wrap, leaving my right arm and hand free to finish the postmortem shooting I had started.

I picked up my .38 from the chair and placed it in the hand of the second torpedo I had shot. We pulled the trigger in the direction of Macella. We were close enough that the bullet hit Jake the Snake and the body twitched a little from the impact.

Using my white handkerchief, I removed the .38 from the shoulder holster of the torpedo who had just fired the slug into his boss. Wiping it clean, I planted it in the hand of clean-cut, who no longer looked clean-cut.

I took clean-cut's .38 from his shoulder holster and, after wiping it, put it in the shoulder holster of the guy who had just shot his boss. I figured it was a fair trade.

I didn't know whether this would be added up by the cops to an internal disagreement among Macella's boys, but it would sure as hell confuse them. With blood and bullets all over the place, with all kinds of people doing the shooting, it would be interesting, to say the least, when they tried to unravel what had happened. If they took blood samples, some of mine might be mixed in, but I hoped to be far away and totally unconnected to the case.

I waited at the door of the liquor store, making sure the sidewalk was clear in both directions before I left. A guy holding a hand over a bloody arm wrapped in a flag could attract attention. I had held the arm tight since coming out of the upstairs room. I had added my white handkerchief under my hand. Between the white shirt I was wearing, the brown sports coat, the tightly wrapped flag, and the white handkerchief my right hand was pressing to the wounded left arm, I was hoping for enough absorption and decreased blood flow to not drip. I didn't want the cops finding a trail of blood that would tell them someone else had been in on the shooting and left alive.

Making the holding of the arm difficult was the fifth of bourbon I had hooked into the bend in my right arm. I was holding it by pressing it to my chest. The bourbon was making the exit difficult, but it would be useful for medicinal purposes while I was on the road.

The sidewalk was clear as I walked at a normal pace toward the Ford. When I got to it, I risked dripping blood by sitting the bourbon down on the street while I unlocked and opened the car door. I was hoping that if anyone observed me they would take me for a drunk who had just got resupplied. With the way I had been holding myself as I had moved down the street and the pain I was experiencing from the bullet wound, the bottle of bourbon in plain sight was probably the best cover I could have.

I was close to Harrisburg, Pennsylvania when I stopped the Ford and opened the fifth. The bourbon burned into the wound as I soaked the flag that was still wrapped around my arm. I had done a good job of stopping the bleeding, and the burning sensation of the bourbon added little to the pain I was already experiencing. I wanted to use the bourbon to sterilize the wound, but I didn't want to waste it all on the wound. It was a long way home and I wanted the comfort of a little drinking to ease the pain. Drinking and driving was not safe, but under the circumstances, I thought it was justified.

It was a long trip that seemed even longer. When getting gas, I covered my blood-soaked arm with my spare sports coat that I had retrieved from my suitcase. All I had to say to the station attendant was, "Fill it up," which required a minimum of contact.

I bought three cans of Spam at a filling station that also ran a little grocery store. The Spam, the bourbon, and the carton of six Coca Cola bottles I bought carried me back to Denver. Eating the Spam with the bottle opener was less than proper etiquette, but since I slept in the car for two nights, it went with the overall pattern of the return journey.

The only really bad part of the trip back was the sweating dreams of Korea. My buddies were dying and the Gooks were bayoneting my arm. I was screaming at my men to move out, but we couldn't move in the sticky blood that was flowing up to our knees. And the whole time my arm hurt like hell.

Eighteen

It was shortly after 9 o'clock at night when I pounded on the door of Dr. Winterlund's house. He worked out of his home on Sheridan Boulevard near Sloan's Lake. His usual office hours were held in the front part of the house that he have converted into a clinic, complete with examining table, medicine cabinets and surgical instruments.

Dr. Winterlund was the kind of a doctor you could trust. He had been an old-time country doctor and the city had just grown up around him. In his early sixties, he still seemed to have the stamina of a young man, even though he was overweight and puffed a pipe nearly constantly. He wasn't overly fond of the spending habits of the federal government and it wouldn't have surprised me to find that he shaved a little off his income tax bill with undeclared income. This was none of my concern--what mattered to me was that he was what I thought a medical doctor should be--a doctor who had compassion for the suffering of the ill and treated them no matter what.

"Martin Mayfield, is that you?" he said, looking at me in the bright light he had turned on before opening the door. "I heard you were back from the Marines."

"Hi, Doc; it's me. How are you?"

"I'm fine, but you don't look like you are in the best of shape. Come on in and let's take a look."

He was smoking his pipe. It smelled like his usual brand of Prince Albert. With his shaggy white hair he looked like Santa Clause, minus a beard. Since office hours were over, he had removed his white medical coat. He was dressed in brown corduroy slacks and a plaid shirt.

"I'm just a little tired, Doc," I said as I went inside and sat down on the examining table where I knew he would want me.

He unwrapped the blood-soaked flag from my arm and had me remove my sports coat and white shirt, both of which would no longer be a part of my wardrobe because of the bloodstains and holes.

"Gunshot wound," Doc Winterlund said as he began to inspect and clean the wound. "You're lucky you got the bleeding stopped. You lose a lot of blood?"

"Some."

"Well, we'll fix you up. After the wound is sterilized and bandaged, a shot in the butt to get rid of the infection and you should be on the mend. You are lucky the bullet went straight through. This related to Frank Brodrick's murder? I heard you were working on the case."

"How did you hear that?"

"I treat everybody, Marty. When you kicked one of those

North-Denver boys in the face at the cemetery, they thought you might have given him a concussion."

"Did I?"

"No."

"How did you know it was me?"

"When they said it was a smart-ass private detective at Frank Brodrick's funeral, I thought you were the most-likely candidate. Supposedly, you kicked him for no reason at all, that right?"

"Yeh, the guy is a Catholic priest and while we were praying together at Frank's funeral my foot accidentally bumped him."

"Sounds like an accident to me," Doc Winterlund said with a smile. "Stand up, turn around and get your pants down. I would have liked to have made Frank's funeral myself, but I was delivering a baby at the time."

"Those needles still as long as ever?" I asked while preparing myself for the shot by leaning forward.

"Longer," Doc Winterlund said as he stuck me. I said nothing while the penicillin was draining from the syringe. My rear was temporarily competing with my arm in the pain department.

"That bandage needs regular changing. If the arm looks like it is acting up, come back and see me. We'll give you another shot in the butt."

"Thanks, Doc, just what I need."

"I think it will be fine. It's healing nicely. You must have been sterilizing the wound. From the smell of the flag you had wrapped around it, I would say whiskey. What were you doing with a flag on it?"

"You don't want to know. Was Frank Brodrick your friend?"

"He was. I ate at the Pig and Poke frequently."

"I know; so just keep your mouth shut about this. You will be doing me and Frank a favor."

"Enough said, Marty."

He saw me trying to decide what to do about the blood-stained shirt and sports coat. "I'll get you a shirt of mine."

"Won't be necessary, Doc. I've got another one in the car."

"I'll burn these," he said, picking up the shirt and sports coat. "Burning is the proper way to dispose of a flag that is no longer going to be used. You want me to burn it?"

"It did its duty, Doc. Put it to rest."

I watched him go into the adjoining room and toss the sports coat and shirt onto the burning logs in the fireplace. Before burning the flag, he folded it neatly and then dropped it gently into the flames.

When he came back to where I was I said, "Thanks, Doc. How much do I owe you?"

"Nothing. As I said, Frank was my friend."

"Thanks, Doc; I appreciate it."

He watched from the door as I went bare-chested into the cold, clear night, opened the door of the Ford, and got in. I pushed the starter button on the dash and the motor of the Ford rumbled to life.

"It's O.K., Doc; I'll put on a shirt when I get home. This Ford has got a good heater."

"Get some sleep too!" he called.

"You can bet on it!" I said as I spun the Ford around and started for Joe Galliger's. Joe would be pleased. I was returning the Ford without a design change.

He was so pleased that he said twice, "My cream puff, a little dirty, but still a cream puff."

It was only after walking around the car while checking it out carefully that he noticed I was shirtless and had a bandaged arm.

"What happened, Marty?"

"I was playing strip poker with a midget and he bit me on the arm."

"Really?"

"No, not really, but that is all you need to know. That is all you want to know, and that is all I'm going to tell you."

"Rough caper, huh, Marty?"

"Rough, Joe, but at least your cream puff is still a cream puff."

"Still a cream puff," he said with satisfaction.

Nineteen

After sleeping most of the next day I met Harry and Delana at the Buffalo Exchange for dinner. The Buffalo Exchange was downtown and fairly close to their work locations, so I thought it was a good choice.

The Buffalo Exchange was a little too Western for Harry. Even though he liked to pretend he knew a lot about the Stock Show and animals, he was a transplanted Easterner. Places that are authentically Western usually make Easterners uneasy, unless they are looking at them on a postcard or watching some portrayal of the West that never was the way the West really was.

The Buffalo Exchange was little more gritty than the

places Delana usually frequented, but if she could tolerate the Red Horse with me, she would have little trouble in adjusting to the Buffalo Exchange because it was infinitely more elegant than the Red Horse.

The Buffalo Exchange was my kind of place--good bourbon, good steaks, historical flair--a room devoted to Buffalo Bill Cody, containing some of the items he had owned and other Western artifacts. I could almost feel the ghost of Buffalo Bill watching me enjoy bourbon and water and a thick steak in a place that was one of his watering holes when he was in the mood to knock back a few, which they say he usually was.

"You ought to have a buffalo burger," I joked with Harry, knowing it was something that would not appeal to him. He didn't know I was joking and shook his head while concentrating on the menu. He settled for beef ribs and baked beans. Delana had mountain trout and I ordered the biggest steak on the menu. I asked for medium-well, knowing that if I ordered it well-done, which I did in most places, it would come out charred. Authentic Western cooking usually burned the hell out of steaks, probably as a result of the influence of the Old West cattle drives that originated in Texas. The texans I had come across in my life considered raw any steak that was not burned black.

We were sitting at a round table with Delana sitting between Harry and me. I had purposely seated myself with my left arm away from them and I didn't think they suspected that my arm was bandaged under the open-necked white shirt and chocolate-brown sports coat I had just bought at Montgomery Wards. My taste in clothes must have not improved any, since neither of them commented on the sports coat--but, since they didn't say anything, I figured it hadn't gotten any worse either.

"What are you going to tell us about it?" Harry asked.

"What?" I asked, doubting that he meant the sports coat.

"Back East, what went on? Five mobsters were rubbed out. I don't suppose you had anything to do with it."

"Not a thing. What did the papers say?"

"The papers said it was a shoot-out among New York gangsters. They think the mobsters had a falling out of some kind and started popping each other. By the time it was over, Jake the Snake Macella's gang had a big hole in it."

"What do the New York cops say?"

"Same thing."

"Well, there you have it. Who are we to question the cops, of which you are a proud member, or the papers, of which Delana is a proud reporter? I'm just a poor private eye from a hick town."

Harry looked over the rib he was holding with two fingers. For a guy originally from the East, I thought he was doing pretty well at eating with his fingers. He was becoming a good Westerner. "Is that what he called you, a hick?"

"Who?"

"Macella."

"If I would have seen or talked to Macella, that is the type of thing he probably would have said. It is just too bad those sophisticates had a disagreement and knocked each other off. Us hicks in the West will never understand their behavior."

Delana reached her left hand over to my right wrist, which had paused in shoveling in the steak long enough to go for a drink from the water glass. "I'm glad you are back safely, Marty."

"Thanks, sweetheart. Too bad other people don't feel that way."

Harry put down the rib he had been gnawing. "I didn't say I wasn't glad you were back safe. I am. I was just seeing if there are any loose ends we have to tie up. Anything you want to tell me or think I should know, Marty?"

"No."

"That's good enough for me. Case closed."

"Not quite. Did you get anything on Fat Georgie?"

"I'm working on it, but nothing definite."

"That's what I thought. I've got an idea, if you and Delana go for it."

Delana frowned and said, "The last time I helped you with a case I almost got killed and ended up walking through the woods in my bra. I hope you can do better this time, darling."

"I can. This time you cover up instead of exposing yourself. Ever dress up as a nun?"

"My background is Protestant. Are you sure I'm right for the part?"

"Harry would make a very silly nun, so I think we ought to stick with you."

"Very funny," Harry broke in. "If you are putting Delana in danger like you did on that Irene Hampton case, I'll have no part of it." He paused as if waiting for a rebuttal or denial from me. When I said nothing, he continued, "Well, let's hear it." I knew from the sound of his voice that any reservations he had about Delana playing the part of a nun would be easily overcome if it meant nailing Fat Georgie for Frank Brodrick's murder.

"Delana and Lucile Brochetti, alias Lucile Brodrick, have a resemblance to each other. They are both about the same height, weight, and build."

"How do you know?" Delana interrupted.

"I did question the girl in L.A."

"Is that all?" Delana asked.

"More or less."

"I thought you said she was very young."

"Who will know under the nun's habit whether she's young or old?"

It wasn't coming out right and I was digging myself in. I wanted Delana to think that Lucile was young, but that she--Delana--was not old.

"How old is she?" Delana asked.

"Twenty-seven, but a young twenty-seven."

"Meaning that I'm an old thirty-three."

"No, I didn't mean it that way. It's just that to me, twenty-seven is like a kid; thirty-three is a real woman."

Harry chuckled. "You're thinking like a married man, Marty. So, why does Delana need to dress up as a nun?"

"Our local mob thinks Lucile Brodrick knows something or has something they want. Why else would they be after her? She doesn't know what it is, but they don't know that she doesn't know. Delana, acting as Lucile, calls Fat Georgie and arranges a meet."

"That's crazy," Harry said. "Why would Lucile do that? That would just make her a sitting duck!"

"Not necessarily. She tells them she has hired a private detective to protect her and that he will be coming to the meeting. I go with her to protect her. They don't know that you and any cops you bring along will be an unseen back-up."

"But why would I give them the information or whatever it is I have?" Delana asked. "Isn't it to Lucile's advantage to stay away from them and turn the information or whatever it is she has on them over to the police?"

"It would be if Lucile knew what it was they thought she had on them. You are going to act as if you--Lucile--do know, and you are going to suggest over the telephone, meeting and trading it for, shall we say, ten-thousand dollars."

"Great, Marty, they show up with ten grand, but Delana doesn't have anything to tell them."

"We stall them, finding out what it is they think Lucile has. We play for time to go get it or to think about the deal."

"What if they try to take you and Delana out right there?"

"I'm there to protect her. You are within visual range. If anything goes wrong, you and I both lay down our lives for Delana."

"Don't sound so melodramatic, Marty," Delana said. "I'm not sure I like the idea of dressing up as a nun and risking getting shot."

"Even for the big story?" I countered. "This is it, and if we nail Fat Georgie and the mob, you can print it all. I honestly don't think that there will be that much danger. I'll be there and Harry and his boys will be in visual contact. They think you have something they want or that you know something they don't want disclosed. If you were going to disclose it without making anything out of it, you would have disclosed it already. Ten grand isn't much to ask them for their peace of mind. They will think you are a greedy nun who wants to cash in on your father's death. That's the kind of logic they will understand."

"It has possibilities," Harry said approvingly. "If Delana calls them and they go for a meet, where do you have in mind?"

"The empty arena of the Denver Coliseum. They are familiar with the place, having bumped off two guys there. As long as we stay out of the tunnel, we are O.K. You can have your men concealed in the announcer's booth, or up in the stands, or anyplace else that you think is wise. That announcer's booth at the edge of the arena is a good place to see any action that occurs in the arena--that's why it is where it is. Using the microphone system of the place, you can be in contact with them at any time you choose."

"And I'm to call this Fat Georgie, say I'm Lucile Brodrick, tell them I want to exchange what they want for ten-thousand dollars and ask them to meet me in the arena at the Denver Coliseum?"

"Four P.M. on the day after tomorrow. O.K. , Harry?" I asked.

"Good. It will give me plenty of time to think and set up."

"What about me?" Delana asked. "Are you sure 4 P.M.

is a good time for me? It would be nice if somebody asked me. After all, I've got to get my nun's act together."

I smiled. "Isn't she wonderful, Harry? I like a women with a little fire."

"Easy, old buddy; she may burn your ego down."

"Ah, but it's worth it," I said.

That night it was worth it when I stayed at her apartment. I dodged questions about the arm, but I told her in tender terms how much she meant to me. I really didn't think anything would happen to her at the meeting with Fat Georgie. Tagging any gangster in the world was not worth putting one little scratch on her beautiful body.

Twenty

Delana and I arrived at the Denver Coliseum at exactly 4 p.m. I could see no one waiting in the arena for us as we descended the cement steps and landings. I could not see anybody anywhere else in the stadium. I knew Harry and any cops he had brought with him must be concealed someplace and that they had done an effective job of hiding themselves.

"Watch your step, Sister," I said, grasping Delana's arm to keep her from tripping on her way down the steps. She was dressed as a nun in a black habit. I was dressed as myself, wearing my usual slacks, sports coat and open-collared white shirt. Today, my slacks were navy blue and my sports coat was tan.

"I don't think I was intended for this type of clothing," she complained. "I think I got it a little too long."

"Don't all nun's habits drag the floor?" I said while searching the arena with my eyes.

"Not as much as mine. I thought if I got it too short it would be a giveaway that I was not a nun. I think I overdid it."

When we reached the arena floor I looked up into the stands and did a complete turnaround. Still no sign of anyone.

"Over there," Delana said, tugging at my arm and directing my attention to where Fat Georgie and his usual two soldiers had just stepped out of the tunnel. He motioned for us to come to them. I thought of making them come to us, but I didn't want to arouse any suspicions about our intentions. Delana and I walked toward them, her nun's habit dragging in the brown dirt of the arena floor as we went.

"Fat Georgie, this is Sister Lucile Brochetti," I said to Fat Georgie and his two torpedoes who had moved to the right of the tunnel entrance.

"Yeh, Mayfield, I know who she is. Where is it?"

"What", I asked.

"What we came to trade for. Al, show 'em the money."

One of the hoods reached into his suit-coat pocket and pulled out a small roll of bills. It only took ten-one-thousand-dollar bills or 100 one-hundred-dollar bills to make ten grand, so I had little doubt that they had actually brought the money.

"How do we know that you won't try to harm Sister Brochetti after she gives you what you want?"

"Did you have to bring him, Sister? What do you want with a smart mouth like Mayfield?" Fat Georgie paused long enough to scowl at me. "He's just a no-account private dick who is trying to do your talking and thinking. Just hand over your father's notarized statement and we will conclude our business."

Delana was keeping her face well back in the hood of her robe. When Fat Georgie and his pals had tried to hustle Lucile into their car at the cemetery, they must have gotten a look a Lucile's face, but in the confusion of the moment, I didn't think they would remember just what they had seen. They showed no signs of thinking that the nun standing before them was anyone other than Lucile Brochetti.

"We didn't bring it," I said.

"What?" Fat Georgie growled. "You want to deal and now you don't want to deal. What is this?"

"I'm just trying to insure protection for Sister Brochetti. I thought we would take you to it so that you don't try to blow her away as soon as she hands it over."

"Where is it?" Fat Georgie was not pleased, but he didn't seem overly angry.

"Go ahead, Sister, tell them where it is," I said, knowing that Delana was cleaver enough to come up with someplace that sounded convincing, and that they were more likely to believe her than me.

"Will we be safe if I tell them?"

"That's up to Fat Georgie. What do you say, Fat Georgie?"

"Sure, you'll be safe. I give you my word."

"It is in a rented locker at the train station."

"Which locker?"

"She's not telling you that until we get there," I threw in quickly.

"That's all we need," a voice said as a figure emerged from the tunnel with a double-barreled shotgun leveled at Delana and me. I had been wondering about the fifth set of footprints found at the scene of Frank Brodrick's murder. The five sets of footprints had belonged to Fat Georgie, his two soldiers, Frank, and a fifth person. The same had been true for the murder of Paulie Lovatto. I was surprised that the fifth set of footprints belonged to Captain Don Garret of the

Denver Police Department. Harry Makris had been right in his suspicions of his police captain. Garret was wearing a dark-gray suit. His blond crew-cut, bull neck, and flat nose reminded me of my Marine Corps drill instructor, which is a face no Marine ever forgets.

"So, you're on Sam Vitaliano's payroll," I said.

"How did you guess, dumbo? I never did like you, and now we are going to take care of you once and for all."

"Aren't you forgetting something?" I asked. "There is still Frank Brodrick's notarized statement that you don't have yet."

"We will. You should know that as a policeman and head of a detective division I can search those lockers anytime I want, without attracting any attention. We don't need you and the sister anymore."

"How about copies?" I asked. "You don't think we would have just one copy of a thing like that."

"Copies won't stand up in court, dumbo. Once we get the statement and see whose notary seal is on it, we make sure the notary doesn't talk. No more Lucile Brochetti; no more notarized statement that names names and dates; and no more dumb private dick named Martin Mayfield."

"Come on," Fat Georgie said impatiently. "We are wasting time. Let's get 'em in the tunnel and get it done unless we have to do them here."

"Throw down your weapon and get your hands up!" Harry Makris' voice boomed over the P.A. "It's all over, Garret, for you and the others. We've got you covered with high-powered rifles."

As soon as I saw Fat Georgie reach for his shoulder holster I knocked Delana to the dirt, falling on top of her. A shotgun blast spreads over its target, but if you are close enough to it, the buckshot doesn't have time to spread much before it reaches the target. Fortunately, Delana and I were close enough to Captain Garret when he fired at us that the blast went over us.

Fat Georgie was hit by a rifle bullet as soon as his pistol cleared the holster. Harry stood up from the announcer's booth that was a quarter of a turn around the arena from the tunnel. He fired his rifle at Garret who had become a moving target running into the tunnel.

Harry missed Garret and I barked to Delana, "Stay down!"

I took off after Garret. The other two torpedoes had their pistols drawn and were scrambling into the stands for cover. Just before I entered the tunnel I caught a glimpse of another rifleman at the top of the arena firing quick shots.

The outside battle continued with shooting that sounded like a small-scale war. In the hollow tunnel I yelled, "Hold it, Garret!"

Garret was turning and pulling his revolver from his shoulder holster as I nailed him with two quick blasts from my .38. As he completed his turn, his back slid down the wall as I pumped another slug into him. When he was in a sitting position, his body fell to the side.

I felt his thick neck for a pulse and found none, which didn't surprise me. Three slugs from a .38 that hit vital spots usually leave a guy very dead.

I looked at the streak of blood that Garret had left on the cement tunnel wall when he slid down. The streak was at the pock-marked place where Frank Brodrick had been blasted with a shotgun.

Frank's bloodstains had been cleaned off, as had Paulie Lovatto's. This time, the right bloodstains were on the wall. "For you, Frank, old buddy," I said as I looked at the new decoration of the wall.

There were no gunshots in the arena as I came out. Harry Makris was coming from the announcer's booth. Another plainclothes cop was coming down one of the cement aisles from the top of the arena. It alarmed me when I saw Delana still lying on the ground.

"Delana," I called as I rushed toward her. She started to get up shakily.

"Well, you told me to stay down."

I pulled her to her feet and held her in my arms. "Are you all right?"

"Yes, I think so."

I kissed her.

"Do you always kiss nuns?" Harry asked as he came over with his rifle barrel pointed down at the dirt.

"Only when they are as beautiful as this one," I said before kissing Delana again.

When I finished the kiss I looked at the police officer who now stood beside Harry, holding a similar rifle that was also pointed down at the dirt. "How come you brought so many guys?" I asked.

"You know officer Joe Gallegos, don't you, Marty? He's the only one I knew for sure I could trust. You saw I was right about Garret."

I released Delana and stuck out my hand to Gallegos. "Good shooting, Joe," I said. "Did you take out all three of them or did Harry get lucky and get one?"

Gallego's hand was shaking when I shook it. "It's the first time I ever killed anybody," he offered by way of explanation.

"It never gets easy," I replied.

"You did a good job, Joe," Harry said to Gallegos. Then he said to me, "I did take out one of them. How did you do with Garret?"

"He's in the tunnel, and I don't think you will ever have to worry about him protecting the mob anymore. He is very dead."

"I figured as much when I saw you walk out of the tunnel."

"Did you get any of this on tape?" I asked.

"Sure did. Even if the microphones I've got planted around the edges of the arena didn't pick everything up--which, incidentally, should still be recording--I've got you, the Good Sister, and Gallegos for collaborating witnesses to the shootings. There is plenty of justification for how we handled the situation."

"Her father probably left it in a safe-deposit box," Delana said.

"What?" Harry asked.

"The notarized statement that names names and probably crimes. It only makes sense. All you have to do is bring Lucile to Denver, see if her father left her a safe-deposit box, and my guess is that you will have the thing that they were so worried about her revealing."

"Where did you get the idea of a locker at the train station?" I asked.

"I saw it in a movie. Gangsters are always leaving things in train-station or bus-station lockers in the movies. Pretty good, huh?"

"Good enough for me," I said. "Maybe that's where it really is, instead of a safe-deposit box."

"Not a chance," Delana said.

Twenty-one

It was a safe-deposit box, just as Delana had thought. The notarized statement, signed by Frank Brodrick, did name names and crimes. Jake the Snake Macella, deceased as he was, and Sam Vitaliano, alive as he was, were highly incriminated. Frank, Paulie, and Carlo were not the only ones who had been in the New York mob. Sam Vitaliano had been in on the hit that had taken out Joe the Boss Masseria. Frank had left behind enough incriminating names, dates, and places to nail Vitaliano for a number of crimes. It was Frank's insurance policy on his life, and Harry let me accompany him and his fellow police officers when we went to pay the policy off to the beneficiary Sam Vitaliano.

It was 12:30 p.m. when Harry's unmarked black Ford and four black and whites abruptly stopped in front of Vitaliano's Restaurant and Lounge. Harry had explained to me on the way over when I had ridden with him that we were making the raid at the lunch hour because that was the time he could be most certain Sam Vitaliano would be there. He would have preferred a time when the restaurant was less-crowded, but he wanted to make sure that Sam Vitaliano was present the first time an arrest was attempted so that Vitaliano wouldn't skip out.

Harry led the way with his service revolver in his right hand and his police badge displayed in his left hand. Eight uniformed officers followed him, half of them carrying rifles at the ready and the other half with drawn revolvers. Since one man from each squad car carried a rifle and the other man from the car carried a pistol, it was an alternating pattern of rifle and pistol.

The move from the front door through the restaurant was made so quickly that many of the restaurant patrons were unaware of the invasion. A few became alarmed enough to rush out the front door. I saw the whole thing clearly because I was at the tail end of the entering officers, figuring it was Harry's show and that I was merely there as a spectator and probably unneeded back-up.

Vitaliano's social secretary, who stood guard as we entered the lounge through the hanging multicolored bead-string curtain, didn't have time to get off his stool before Harry said, "Police. Move it! Let's go see Mr. Vitaliano." The burly door guard looked startled but moved quickly without comment, leading the way across the lounge and through the wooden, saloon swinging doors into Vitaliano's dining room.

"Police!" Harry yelled as the officers entered the dining room and quickly spread out around the table with weapons leveled at Sam Vitaliano's's dinner guests. I was surprised that with the elimination of Fat Georgie and his two soldiers, the table was just as full as it had been the last time Harry and I had visited Sam Vitaliano. Apparently, there was no shortage of recruits for organized crime.

"What is the meaning of this?" Sam Vitaliano asked calmly as he looked up and put his dinner fork beside his half-eaten plate of spaghetti. The others stopped eating also. Vitaliano looked the same as the last time I had seen him. He still had a cue-ball head with a string of hair across the top of it.

"Mr. Vitaliano, you are under arrest," Harry said calmly.

"For what?" Vitaliano asked indignantly.

"Well, for one thing, Mr. Vitaliano, murder. For another, illegal gambling. Do you want to hear more?"

"Ridiculous. I'm a legitimate businessman."

"A businessman, yes; legitimate, no."

"I've got my rights," Vitaliano protested. "You can't arrest me. I'll have your head for this. I know people."

"Come on, Vitaliano," Harry said, his voice rising in anger. "You're just a punk who made it to the big time. Get up and face the wall before I lose my patience."

Harry assisted Vitaliano in making the move by grabbing the collar of Vitaliano's black suit coat and pulling him up from the chair. Harry shoved him against the wall and kicked his legs apart.

As Harry patted Vitaliano down and handcuffed his hands behind him, Vitaliano said, "You're not a real Italian, just a half-breed Greek who is going to get his ass burned."

When Harry had him cuffed, he put his mouth close to Vitaliano's left ear. I couldn't understand what he was saying in a quiet, measured tone, but I knew it was Italian from the sound of the words. I could tell be the faces of the table guests that whatever Harry was saying it wasn't nice.

Harry's ability to speak more than one language surprised me, although it shouldn't have. Harry had a way of surprising you with things that you never expected. He never mentioned something, and you would go along for years never knowing it was there, and then out it popped. I wondered if Harry also spoke Greek.

"You may resume your meal, gentlemen," Harry said in English as he pushed Vitaliano in front of him and he and Vitaliano started toward the wooden, saloon swinging doors. "You may want to think about this," he continued. "This is where a life of crime leads."

Several of the table guests uttered words that I took to be Italian profanity. Harry laughed and uttered something back in Italian. As Vitaliano went by me he said, "You will pay for this, private dick. You will be taken care of."

"He doesn't like private detectives," I said as I fell in behind Harry. I didn't want to be the last one to exit the room. I figured that was the cops' job. I was merely an observer, and if anybody started shooting, I hoped it wouldn't be at me.

"So I noticed," Harry replied.

About half of the patrons of the dining room had vanished during our brief encounter in the back room. Those remaining sat in silence and watched Sam Vitaliano being escorted out of his restaurant in handcuffs. From a business standpoint, this probably wasn't too good.

Vitaliano was deposited in the back of one of the black and whites for the ride downtown. I had less faith in the court system than Harry did, but I didn't say so as I rode downtown with Harry in the unmarked black Ford. Why should I rain on his parade? I helped him enjoy his triumph, agreeing with him about how great it was to take Sam Vitaliano down.

Personally, I preferred putting the bad guys into coffins rather than handcuffs, but this was Harry and the law. Maybe smart lawyers wouldn't get Vitaliano off and maybe Vitaliano would go down. When I put them down, I knew they were down.

"You know we've both got to be extra careful," Harry said. "We are both probably going to be on the MAFIA's hit list, if we are not already on it."

"Why would you think that, Harry? After all, all we did was take out Fat Georgie, two torpedoes, a police captain who was on the mob payroll, get evidence to prosecute mob figures, and now we are locking up a mob boss. What makes you think that would make organized crime unhappy with us?"

Harry smiled. "But it sure feels good, doesn't it?"

"Sure does," I agreed, but I would have felt better if we had put Sam Vitaliano in a coffin rather than in a jail cell.

Twenty-two

We gathered at the Red Horse for a postmortem of the case I called "Homecoming to Murder'. I liked to give all my cases names, analyze them, and file them away in memory.

The gathering was my idea. I thought it would help Delana write her story for the newspaper. I also thought it would be good for Lucile to know all of the facts surrounding her father's death. For Harry and me it was an excuse to have drinks in the company of two beautiful women. With Beverly serving us, I figured it for three beautiful women.

The weather at 7 p.m. was frigid cold. Snow was blowing outside the Red Horse, but inside it was warm. On a Tuesday night, we were practically the only ones there. A few of the regulars were saddled up to the bar, talking to Beverly as they drank, but most had stayed home to skip the storm. After about ten minutes of pleasant conversation I focused the conversation on the case by bringing up the attire Lucile and Delana had worn.

"It's nice to get you ladies out of those nun's habits," I said. "You were attractive as nuns, but I think I like you better this way."

Delana and Lucile were both wearing slacks and sweaters, which was a bit unusual for Delana. Considering the cold, Delana's wearing of slacks was understandable. I didn't know what Lucile normally wore in cold weather, but I thought her purple knit sweater and gray slacks were attractive. Delana could never wear anything that didn't look attractive. Her blue cashmere sweater and black slacks accented her usual beauty.

Delana and Lucile were sitting across from Harry and me in the booth. I had arranged it that way as we sat down, not wanting to show preference to either lady by sitting with one over the other. Harry faced Lucile on the inside of the booth and I faced Delana on the outside. Delana had a note pad and pen in front of her because this was a working session for her.

"Why the nun's garb?" Delana asked Lucile.

"My background in the Catholic school and my father's warning to me that if I ever came to Denver to be especially careful."

"Your father was a member of the New York prohibition gangs," Delana said, less-than-sensitive to Lucile's feelings. The reporter in her was on the prowl. "What can you tell me about what he did when he was in the MAFIA?"

I took over in an attempt to spare Lucile's feelings. "Yes, Frank was in the MAFIA, but he reformed a long time ago. He took Lucile to California to the Catholic girls' school and he led a decent life to the very end."

Delana ignored me. "How do you feel about your father's

death?"

"How would you feel?" Lucile shot back. "I feel very bad. He was extremely good to me. He was the only known relative I had. Wouldn't you feel bad if it were your father who had been killed by gangsters?"

I tried to reassert myself into the conversation. "First, the Feds squeezed Frank to testify. Then the mob retaliated. Fat Georgie tried to grab Lucile at the funeral and I entered the case."

"That's one way of saying it," Harry said. "I would say you nearly kicked Georgie and his cronies' teeth out."

Delana continued her questioning. "How do you feel about what you did to Fat Georgie at the cemetery and later what ultimately happened? Any remorse, Marty?"

"None. No regrets. No sympathy for Fat Georgie or any of the mob. Fat Georgie got what was coming to him and I'm glad I had a part in delivering him his due."

"When you went to New York and came back from there, what went on?"

"None of your business," I said.

Harry said, "You know what the papers say, Delana. Marty had nothing to do with what went on in New York. Some mobsters happened to shoot each other while he was back there. He had nothing to do with it. If you value Marty's life, you won't mention anything about his trip to New York."

The reporter within Delana struggled with the woman in her, but only for a second. Then she said, "O.K., no mention of Marty's trip to New York. What about his trip to California?"

"That's O.K. to print," I said. "I tracked Lucile through the girls' school. I put her in a safe house with one of her friends and came back to Colorado. Nothing much to write about that."

"That's all?" Delana asked as if she was not convinced.

"That's all," Lucile said.

I liked my women discreet. If it was one thing I didn't like, it was a woman who talked after sharing my body. So, I had gone to bed with Lucile and rubbed out three members of the mob while in California--that was Lucile's and my secret.

Beverly interrupted by bringing us our second round of drinks. Beverly was wearing a rich red sweater and gold slacks. She brushed against me as she sat Harry's bottle of Coors in front of him.

In the presence of so much femininity, it made me glad to think that I had been a part of these ladies' lives. Harry's dream for me of settling down in suburbia with a wife completely faded from my mind when I was in their collective presence.

It was only when I was with them individually or thought about them individually that thoughts of domesticity overtook me. I could see myself sharing an apartment or track home with Delana in Denver. I could see myself living in a beach house with Lucile, opening onto the vast expanse of the turquoise Pacific in California. Beverly's house trailer didn't even look bad, even though she had rung up a few more years than I had. It was good that the three of them were getting together with me like they were in the present situation--it kind of brought me to my senses about domesticity.

Delana interrupted my thoughts by saying, "The contents of the safe-deposit box, how incriminating were they?"

"Very," Harry replied. "I don't want to give you specifics of what was in it. Let's just say the Frank named enough names, dates, and crimes to make a good case against Sam Vitaliano and some other organized-crime figures."

"May I quote you on the shooting at the Denver Coliseum, Harry. Was the shooting justified and could it have been handled in any other way?"

"Sure, you can quote me," Harry said, seeming flattered

at the thought of his opinion being in a newspaper story. "It was absolutely justifiable the way we handled it. It was a textbook case of the police, the press--you, and a private citizen--Martin Mayfield, working in harmony to bring to justice violators of law and order."

"Sounds pretty good," I said with a slight chuckle. "Be sure, Delana, to mention how part of the police was on the take and that Captain Garret cooperated by getting shot. Don't forget to mention the time that you spent lying in the dirt."

"I will take full credit for wearing that nun's robe. Lucile and I both deserve special recognition for that. Those poor nuns, they probably get used to it, but they deserve any and all credit for wearing them."

"I may be wearing one permanently," Lucile said tentatively.

"Really?" Delana said, expressing the surprise of all of us.

"I need time to think about it. I haven't made up my mind yet, but I'm leaning that way. The death of my father made me think about how short life really is. Maybe I'm ready to enter the order now."

"Good for you, kid," I said, but I wasn't sure I meant it. "What are you going to do about the Pig and Poke?"

"I'm keeping it, even though I'm going back to California. Ida will run it. We've already agreed on everything. It will just go on as before, except for my father not being there."

I could see sadness in Lucile's eyes and I knew she would miss the visits of her father. "I miss your father too," I said, trying to console her.

"Oh I almost forgot." Lucile started to dig in her black purse. "This was also in the safe-deposit box." She handed me a white envelope with the words MARTY MAYFIELD on it.

I opened the envelope and counted thirty-six fifty-dollar bills.

"I knew Frank was a straight shooter and would save the money for me I sent him while I was in the Marines. He gave me good advice, telling me to put a few bucks aside so that I wouldn't end up, as he put it, a stumblebum. Your father was O.K."

"I hate to break this up," Harry said, "but I've got to get home to the wife and kids. Why don't you come along, Marty? You still haven't seen the kid I named after you."

"Don't's you need to call your wife first, to make sure it's O.K.?" I asked.

I could see by their looks that Lucile and Delana approved of my being considerate of Harry's wife.

"No. I figure this is the only way you are going to take time to see him. We'll just pop in and surprise her."

Delana and Lucile frowned at Harry.

"Some people are just inconsiderate," I said as I got up to leave with Harry. "You ladies want us to drop you anyplace on the way?"

"Won't be necessary," Delana answered. "If we go anyplace, we will take a cab. I want to chitchat with Lucile for awhile, if she doesn't mind. No more about the case, woman-to-woman stuff. I wouldn't want Lucile to go back to California without feeling that we are hospitable in Denver. I think we all need to relax a little after what we have been through."

"If any guys try to pick you up, yell for Beverly," I suggested. "She'll help you fend them off."

"Who wants to fend them off?" Lucile said. "I'm not a nun yet."

"After I see Harry's kid, I'll come back. If the two of you are still here, maybe we can figure out something for the rest of the evening."

"What makes you think we'll wait for you?" Delana

asked.

"I might get lucky," I replied.

Delana and Lucile looked at each other and smiled. "Egotistical, isn't he?" Lucile said.

"Very," Delana agreed.

I winked at Beverly as Harry and I went out the door. It was tough work and nobody had to do it, but I sure enjoyed it.

And so the case of 'Homecoming to Murder' came to a close. The octopus of organized crime was still there and would always be there, but Harry and I had cut off a few of its tentacles. They grew back as fast as they were chopped off, but that was the kind of work somebody had to do. If we didn't keep chopping, the American dream would be squeezed to death by corruption.

The Korean War would fade into history, as do all wars. The sacrifices of those who fought there would become a footnote to history. My homecoming to murder would be a thing of the past.

Bad guy Frank Brochetti had become good guy Frank Brodrick before he had passed on. His daughter might or might not become a nun. Harry, Red, Beverly, Joe Galliger, and the rest of us--all of us little people--would go on, doing the things little people do. Delana would write her newspaper stories and I would give her stuff to write by putting down the bad guys. Maybe that was the way it was meant to be. If it wasn't, who would ever know or care?